DESTINY:
Quest For
The Four Elements

by
Elyse M. Redwine

Dedication

Dedicated to my family and the real Shade,
my dog, Charlie.

About The Author

Elyse Marie Redwine was born in New Orleans, Louisiana in 2001. From a very early age, she had an intense love of animals. Almost as soon as she could hold a pencil, she began drawing dogs, cats and horses on any piece of paper she could find. In her early elementary school years, she added short stories about animals to her artwork. It was in her fourth grade year that Elyse began to exhibit a true gift for creative writing. With encouragement from her teachers and family, she has continued to pursue that talent.

"Destiny: Quest For The Four Elements" began as a submission for a short story contest at Elyse's local library entitled, "Destiny Earth: Volume I". She won the contest, but felt there was much more to the story and its characters, so she continued to write.

She is currently in the 6th grade at Eisenhower Elementary School at Ft. Leavenworth, Kansas where she has been an active member of the choir, band (French Horn), and Odyssey of the Mind (two-time Kansas State 1st Place Division One, one-time Kansas State 1st Place Division Two, three-time World Finals Team, Division One/Two and 2011 Kansas State Team OMER Award). Elyse has also been extremely proud to be an "Army Brat".

Elyse lives in Lansing, Kansas with her parents, Jim & Gina Redwine, her older brother, Nicholas, and Charlie, her Golden Retriever, who was her inspiration for this book.

Table of Contents

Destiny

Earth: Volume I

Chapter 1

Shade winced as cold rain pattered on his pelt. Dark clouds circled the city. Though it was night, all stars were hidden and unseen. Only the moon's dull light shone through the gradually thickening storm.

This is stupid, Shade thought. *I need to find shelter.*

Shade stood and steadied himself, only to be knocked over again by a pair of cats.

"Hey, watch it," Shade grunted.

The black tom spoke. The cat beside him was a tabby she-cat. "Watch where you put your paws, dog!"

Shade growled a threat, and the cats scurried into a hole in one of the buildings.

Where Shade stood was a dark alley. Dumpsters lined the walls of the surrounding buildings. Litter lay everywhere, and dips in the asphalt were homes to many puddles. Sand and dirt lay all over the narrow space. Shade heaved himself up once more. Water poured out of his gray and black fur. The mutt sighed.

Rain.

He stepped out of the narrow alley that he called home. Men and women were running home from work. A group of kids ran through the muddied streets, thoroughly soaked. Cars rumbled past, their headlights bright on the dark scene.

A group of dogs galloped by. They barked their arrival. One of the dogs purposefully splashed water in Shade's face.

"Half-mutt!" The dogs barked out Shade's most hated nickname.

"Shut up," Shade growled.

A younger dog in the group strutted up to Shade. "H-A-L-F mutt! Know what that spells?"

Shade only snarled in reply.

"Half-mutt! The young dog yelped, tauntingly. His companions laughed, wagging their tails. They summoned their younger member back.

"Move it, Half-mutt. We're trying to get through, and you're hogging the sidewalk," the leader of the group threatened.

"I think that you can manage going around me just fine, Snag," Shade said.

Snag's fur began to stand up. "What?"

"I said, 'go around'," Shade growled.

Snag snarled, showing row upon row of glistening white teeth. "'Go around' he says. Well, I suppose we'll have to make Half-mutt here understand that going around isn't an option."

Shade stood stock-still. Ooh, he'd gone overboard this time.

The rain seemed to come down harder.

The five dogs following Snag, including the young, taunting one, leaped at Shade. Shade sprang out of the way. The dogs all landed in a heap. Shade sprinted away from the alley opening where the scene had taken place.

A bolt of lightening followed by a clap of thunder brightened the whole city.

Shade made a veering turn into another part of the city. He knew that he had to get away. Suddenly, the same black tom raced past. The two tumbled into each other, hissing and growling. When they finally screeched to a stop, the black tomcat jumped up, fur bristling.

"Are you out of your puny canine mind?" the cat spat.

"Where are you off to in such a hurry, cat?" Shade queried.

"Shelter, you idiot!"

"Where?" Shade asked, hopefully.

"Why do you need to know?" the cat countered, before racing off again.

"Wait!" Shade yelped.

The black cat ran into an alley, leaped onto a dumpster, jumped from it to a clothesline and sprang from a white shirt to the top of a building.

Impressive.

Shade followed along on the ground. He could still see the cat's black tail. The cat turned and looked down at Shade, he scowled. "Quit it!"

"What?" Shade asked.

"Following me!"

Shade flattened back his pointy ears. The cat hissed, and then kept going.

"What's your name, anyway?" Shade asked, after a while of silence.

The cat looked down at Shade, hissing. "You're still following me?"

Shade just looked at him.

"Ugh!" the cat admitted defeat. "My name's Shadow. But everyone calls me Hurricane."

"Who's 'everyone'?" Shade asked.

Hurricane hopped off the roof to the wet sidewalk. It was still raining. "The other alley-cats. They call me Hurricane for my agility. I'm fast, athletic and clever."

This cat really thinks highly of himself, doesn't he?

The cat shot a sideways glance down the sidewalk, then back at Shade. "What happened back there with Snag's group wanting to fight you?" Hurricane asked, surprisingly seeming to be concerned.

"You saw that?" asked Shade.

"We cats see everything. We climb, slink, step quietly, and are really quite clever," Hurricane added with a look of pride.

9

Wow. He really is an arrogant jerk.

"Cool. I guess," Shade said with a shrug.

"So…"

"So… what?" Shade asked.

"The answer to my question!"

"Oh, that," Shade remembered. "You see, I'm not all dog."

Hurricane's head whipped around. "What?"

"I'm part wolf, you know," Shade stated.

"Which parent?" Hurricane asked.

"My father. My mother was a street dog and met him just outside the city."

"Then what brings you to the outskirts of New York?"

"My mother brought me here. She didn't think that the forest was safe," Shade added.

"But how does that connect to the near-fight?" Hurricane pressed.

"The dogs around here don't want a wolf among them. They think I'm different. They make fun of me."

"Is being half-dog, half-wolf why they call you Half-mutt?"

"Yup," Shade said simply.

Hurricane shook his head, disapprovingly. "Idiots."

Shade looked at Hurricane in surprise. He was *sympathizing* with him.

"Er…. thanks, I guess."

Hurricane looked Shade in the eye. "Let's just find that shelter, okay?"

"Okay," Shade agreed.

The two walked on until they came to a rundown, abandoned house.

"This looks stable enough," Shade said.

"I don't care if it'll crash down on us. I just want to get out of this rain," Hurricane meowed.

"Okay. Let's get inside." Shade exclaimed.

Shade walked in first. The door had come off its hinges and was propped up in the doorway. A small space between the door and the wall allowed entry for the two.

"This place looks *awful*," Hurricane commented.

It was. Every window was dusty, and all but one were cracked. The wood of the house was broken and rotting. The chimney's bricks were coming apart. The roof was beginning to fall in. The porch was falling apart. Weeds and piles of wooden planks and bricks were out on the front lawn. Shade took a disapproving glance once more before proceeding inside.

The inside was bleak as well. Old furniture lay in random spots. Broken photos hung loosely from the walls. Broken china and vases lay on the floor and on old coffee tables. The rain dripped through the crumbling roof.

It was frightfully dark.

Shade weaved around unstable upholstery. He stopped on a faded rug.

"Should we even be here?" A voice behind Shade made him jump. He whipped around to find Hurricane's stocky black build before him. Hurricane twitched his white whiskers.

"Don't sneak up on me like that!" Shade exclaimed.

"Sorry," said Hurricane. "I'm going to check out the upstairs."

Hurricane hopped lightly up the unstable set of stairs. He disappeared at the top. Shade sidestepped nervously. He took a deep breath. "Hello? Is anybody here?"

"No."

Shade's heart skipped a beat. His breath got caught in his throat. He looked in the direction of the voice. That *wasn't* Hurricane.

One glowing green eye was illuminated in the shadows. A dog with an eye-patch and scars stepped out of the darkness.

"Only me, Shade."

Chapter 2

"Who are you? How do you know my name?" Shade was still shaking.

"I know a lot of things, Shade. I know true secrets that one could only imagine."

Shade stared blankly into this dog's good eye.

What does he want with me?

"For instance," the dog began, "I know that you are only one half Husky-German Shepherd mix, and also one half wolf."

Shade shuddered. Did *everybody* know his secret? He took a step backwards.

"The name's Everest. Like the mountain," the stranger offered.

This made a bit of sense. He looked about three parts Burmese Mountain Dog. But he had pointy ears and blue eyes, like a Husky.

"What do you want with me, *Everest*?" Shade asked, putting emphasis on the dog's name.

Everest grinned. "Get your little kitty-friend down here first."

"Hurricane!" the two barked at the same time. Shade looked at Everest.

"You know Hurricane's name, too?"

Everest chuckled. "Not only that. I know that his true name is Shadow."

"How? How do you know this?" Shade asked, almost annoyed.

Everest just laughed and held up his paw. It was clasped together. But when he opened it, beautiful blue sparks, like mini fireworks, illuminated the dark room.

"Magic."

Chapter 3

"Magic?" Shade echoed as he, Hurricane, and Everest watched the rainfall from the porch.

Hurricane had come down earlier. He had shrieked at the sight of Everest, almost falling off the stairs. The railing had stopped him. When he calmed down, he was introduced to Everest by Shade.

"Of course. That's why I'm here. That's why you two are here," Everest added.

Shade's jaw dropped. Where was Everest going with all this?

Everest stared at them both, unblinking. "You two have an amazing destiny before you. I'm here to tell you of it."

"Are you mad?" Hurricane asked, sarcastically. "*What* destiny? I have better things to do than listen to your stories."

Years of experience and wisdom twinkled in Everest's good eye. "Better things to do than save the Earth from everlasting darkness?" he asked, raising an eyebrow.

Hurricane stopped walking and whirled around to face Everest. "What now?"

Shade remained silent. Fear welled up inside him at the thought of what Everest called "everlasting darkness".

"*Everlasting darkness*?" Hurricane echoed Everest's bone-chilling words. "What do you mean?"

Everest closed his eyes. He took a breath and sat down. He let the breath out, and a huge gust of wind buffeted everyone's fur. Hurricane hissed.

"I come from a long line of Sighters. Sighters were dogs that began in the mountains, and could hear the wind and water whisper words and secrets of the future in their ears. Each Sighter took on the name of a mountain, since that's where they originated. Generations upon generations of Sighter Dogs spread all around the world, and keep themselves hidden. Once a year, on the night of the Winter Solstice, all the Sighters of the world meet in the Rocky Mountains and exchange news. The reason we Sighters exist is to guard the world from evil

14

darkness that threatens the Earth. Few know this fact, but darkness is found lurking everywhere. In the shadows, in the night, even in the hearts of the people. We Sighters keep the darkness found everywhere from becoming powerful and overwhelming the planet. But, a darkness stronger than any other has risen and threatens our lives." Everest took a breath. "A prophecy was given to all of the Sighters that a cat and a wolf-dog by the names of Shadow and Shade would overcome this darkness. That cat and wolf are you."

Hurricane scored the wooden floor with his claws. "Are there cat Sighters?" he asked.

Everest nodded. "Though the story of how they began has been lost over the years. They are named for the constellations."

"They must have a much wider name choice," Hurricane meowed.

Everest sighed. "A common mistake, no. There are only about 100 constellations and almost 450 mountains. But Sighters are so few in number, it doesn't really matter."

Shade was still confused. "But what do we have to do?"

Everest gazed at Shade. "You must proceed on a quest to find the four elements of the Earth: Earth, Water, Air and Fire."

"A quest. A *quest*. What?" Shade couldn't believe his ears.

"No way!" Hurricane exclaimed. "I'm not going on any quest!"

"Too late," Everest said, solemnly. Before Hurricane could even protest, a flash of light obscured the scene inside of the house.

Chapter 4

Suddenly, the light dispersed and the two found themselves on a hilly landscape. Far off to the east was a small grove of trees. Other than that, there was only grass. All to the north, south and west were grass and hills as far as the eye could see.

"Ugh!" Hurricane exclaimed.

"Earth…. the first element," whispered a voice that echoed in Shade and Hurricane's heads.

Hurricane flickered an ear. "Well, apparently we're looking for earth. Just dirt, right?"

"I don't think it will be that simple, Hurricane," Shade said. "I mean, dirt is all around us. If we just needed any dirt we wouldn't be on a quest."

Hurricane hissed. "Fine, fine, so then what do we do?"

Shade shrugged.

"Hello!" squeaked a small voice.

Shade and Hurricane turned around to find a small black kitten with a white belly and paws.

"This will be your guide to find the first element."

"This pipsqueak? The Sighters seriously couldn't do any better?" Hurricane spat. The kitten looked hurt by Hurricane's rude comment.

"Hurricane!" Shade barked. "Be a little more considerate, will you?"

The kitten spoke up. "I'm Eco! Eco the kitten! I'm here to help you two find the earth element!"

Shade smiled. This kitten was pretty cute. Shade even saw Hurricane crack a small smile.

"Wait, wait! I almost forgot!" the kitten disappeared into the sea of waving green stalks again. When he came back out, he held a small

16

green leather pouch. The pouch had a small green ribbon strung through. A green "E" was embroidered onto the little pouch.

"Do you mind if I hop on your back for a moment Shade?" Eco mumbled, the pouch stuck in his mouth.

"How do you know my name?" Shade asked.

"Everest," was all that Eco said before hopping onto Shade's back. Eco tied the pouch around Shade's neck with the ribbon.

"What exactly is this pouch for, Echo?" Shade asked.

"Eco. My name is Eco, not Echo. Although, Echo does sound cool. You can call me by it if you like."

Shade flicked his ear.

"Oh, right. The pouch is to keep the earth that you collect."

"Okay," Shade replied.

Eco hopped off of Shade's back once the Earth Pouch was tied around Shade's neck. "Perfect! Let's go!" mewed Eco.

Hurricane rolled his eyes. "Can we rest first?"

Shade shot Hurricane an angry glance. "Fine," Hurricane growled with a scowl.

"This way!" Eco mewed before bouncing toward the grove of trees. He waved his tail proudly, leading the way.

Shade liked this little kitten. He was funny. Shade and Hurricane followed along behind. After a while, the three came to a small grove of trees.

"Here we are! C'mon, I'll show you where the Earth Element is!" Eco mewed. Shade followed along. Hurricane stalked after them. "C'mon, come on!" Eco chanted. Eco burst through a row of bushes and disappeared. At first Hurricane and Shade were concerned. They stayed put. "C'mon in!" squeaked a little voice from the other side of the hedges.

"Okay," Shade woofed. "Let's go, Shadow." Hurricane hissed. "Fine. Let's go *Hurricane*."

The two walked through the hedges to find a small clearing with a huge boulder in the middle. At the tip-top of the boulder, a green, glowing ball hovered. Inside the ball, there was a wad of dirt.

"The first element...." The echoing voice whispered in their ears. *"Grasp it. Grasp it."*

"First element. Let's roll, " Shade said coolly.

Hurricane huffed. "You can't do it," he meowed with a laugh.

"Shut up," Shade said with a grin.

The three stepped forward a few paces. "Grab it!" Eco cheered.

"Okay," Hurricane meowed. He hopped onto the boulder. He climbed to the top and looked down at Eco. "Well?"

"Well...what?" Eco asked.

"What do I do?" Hurricane asked.

"Don't ask me! I'm just the guide."

Hurricane slapped a paw over his face. "Seriously?"

Eco crouched down.

"Don't look at the kitten. I'll tell you what to do," said a voice from behind.

Shade and Hurricane jumped. Eco looked expectantly toward the voice that happened to be familiar to him.

The second time today that I've been spooked by an unknown voice, Shade thought.

To Shade and Hurricane's amazement, a blue, green and brown wolf stepped out from the trees. She was like planet Earth in wolf shape. A dull green and blue glow encircled her figure.

Chapter 5

"I am Earth, keeper of the first element." Brown leaves greened at the beautiful tone of her voice. "To collect this element, say the words, 'Earth, the first element'."

Hurricane stared at Earth as though she had grown a second head.

"Do it, Hurricane!" Earth exclaimed.

Without even hesitating to ask Earth about how she knew his name, Hurricane echoed the phrase. "Earth, the first element."

Brilliant green lights illuminated the dark space. The lights were exploding out of the small green globe embracing the wad of dirt. The globe stopped hovering and fell into Hurricane's outstretched paws with a thud.

"Amazing," Hurricane breathed.

"Now take the dirt out of the globe and put it in the Earth Pouch, " Earth instructed. Hurricane hopped down and walked up to Shade who had the pouch strapped around his neck.

"How do I get it out of the globe?" Hurricane asked.

"Put a paw on each end and press. The globe will disappear."

Hurricane nodded and did as he was told. In a flash of green, the globe was gone. A glowing wad of dirt lay in his paws. Hurricane dropped the dirt into the Earth Pouch. The embroidered "E" turned gold and began to glow.

"Every time you collect an element, the embroidered letter will turn gold and glow. If ever you lose an element, the letter goes back to its normal color," Earth explained.

"Okay, " Hurricane and Shade said in unison.

"Well done, you two, " said a voice behind them. The two turned to see Everest standing there. "You have collected the first element. Three to go." With that, Everest disappeared.

"Bye," said Eco reluctantly. He scampered over to Earth's sitting figure. He hid between her two front legs.

"Good luck. Be safe. Peace be with you," Earth said. Just like that, Shade and Hurricane were swept back to the abandoned house.

"Earth," breathed Shade. "Three to go."

Destiny

Air:
Volume II

Chapter 6

Hurricane slipped through a crack in the building wall. Two large toms halted him.

"Halt. What is your name?" the first one asked.

Hurricane rolled his eyes. "You know my name, bone-heads. Let me through."

"It's our job to be told the identification of each cat that comes through this entrance," the second one added, pride seasoning his voice.

Idiots, Hurricane thought.

"Tell us your information, and you will be let through," the first one growled, firmer this time.

"Ugh. Fine. My name is Hurricane."

"Yes, and?" The first tom asked.

"And I am a black tom."

"And?"

"And I… have… lived in this club for longer than I can remember? Seriously, guys, we don't have to go through all this. Just let me in."

"Tell us the password, and you will be let in," the second one meowed.

Hurricane sighed. "Fine then." He tried to remember. "'No club-cat fears the night'. Happy?"

The first cat nodded in approval. "Excellent. You may proceed through the entrance into club's secret fort."

"Finally!" Hurricane hissed. "Thank you, Link." Hurricane nodded to the first tom, which was a large light brown tabby. "Thank you, Jax." Hurricane nodded to the second tom, a smaller black and white tuxedo cat.

Hurricane padded through the crack that had been used as an entrance to the club. The crack led to an old unused storage room at the back of a restaurant. The cats that lived in the club were taking a huge risk, because the restaurant wasn't even vacant. It was really quite a popular New York Italian restaurant.

The storage room had become useless to the restaurant. A new storage room had been built closer to the kitchen. Not only was it more convenient, it was far larger. The old storage room had become forgotten, now becoming a comfortable spot for the club to live. Since the restaurant was still active, it even had an air conditioning and heating unit. There were shelves stacked with food and supplies, enough for every cat to build a steady place to sleep each night. And since there was an alley outside, prey could be easily caught, or trash quickly brought in to be put to good use.

Hurricane weaved in and out through small groups of chatting cats. He grabbed a mouse and a slice of bread from the food stockpile in a cardboard box. He could tell that the bread had been recently taken from the Italian restaurant's kitchen, because it was steaming and still smelled good. The mouse also smelled as though it had been caught sometime today. Hurricane would eat well tonight.

He let himself fall into his bed made of a full flour-sack and an old burgundy hand-towel. He curled up in the large indentation in the flower sack and covered himself in the towel.

He thought back to three nights ago, when he met Shade, the half-wolf-half-dog. He remembered Everest, the scarred mutt with an eye-patch who called himself a Sighter Dog. He remembered being sent to the open field to find the "Earth Element" and meeting Eco, the friendly black and white kitten who acted as their guide to the first element. He especially remembered Earth, a beautiful wolf with the strangest fur pattern. She actually looked like the Earth in the shape of a canine. Hurricane could make out the seven continents and everything!

Hurricane knew that these thoughts were going to prevent any sleep whatsoever.

That was when the beautiful yellow tabby she-cat who was his best friend appeared in the corner of his vision. She had been with him the first time that he came in contact with Shade; the two had gotten tangled in the gray wolf-dog's legs.

"Hi, Hurricane," the yellow tabby said in a friendly tone. "Do you mind if you could make some room for me? Jasmine's kittens stole my bed. I asked them to move, but all they did was get upset and wail for Jasmine to come and make me leave. I wasn't going to take the risk of getting into another, 'they started it, no she started it' argument, so I left." She let her gaze slide down from the head of the sack to the foot of it. She then turned her eyes back to Hurricane. "So? May I sleep in your bed tonight?"

"Sure, Lexie. I don't mind." Hurricane scooted over to make room. He realized that one of his paws was hanging over the side of his flour sack bed. *Oh well.* Lexie fell down beside him. She took one end of the towel and covered herself in it.

"A bit crammed, but," Lexie shuffled again to get comfortable, "it'll do for tonight."

The two lay faced toward each other on their sides. Hurricane's paw was beginning to get cold from resting on the cool wooden floor. "I can't sleep." Hurricane finally mewed.

A cat resting at the top of a wheelbarrow by a shelf near Hurricane and Lexie whipped around in its bed, throwing pawfuls of hay onto a row of resting cats. They all hissed at him. He hissed back, and then turned to the two friends. He curled back his lips, showing a row of glistening white teeth. "Shut up! Some of us are trying to sleep here!" He hissed.

"Exactly!" hissed a white she-cat back to the cat on the wheelbarrow. She lifted from her bed made of a pile of towels and arched her back. "So don't add onto the racket, genius!"

The cat on the wheelbarrow, a yellow tom with black stripes across his back, let out a final hiss then lay down in the hay of the wheelbarrow, out of sight of the other cats. The white she-cat rolled her eyes then settled back down as well.

A group of a few late-nighters at the other side of the room that had been chatting turned around and listened in on all of the commotion. Once the argument finished, they all broke out into a chorus of giggles and laughs.

The bumblebee-striped tom sprang from the wheelbarrow. He sailed over two rows of sleeping cats and landed on all four paws. He stalked angrily over to the groups of cats. They were huddled by a lantern lit with a flame while talking and enjoying some bread and cheese. A few cats scattered at the sight of him, but most stayed, rolled their eyes at the approaching tom, and kept on chatting away.

"You think it's funny?" he hissed. "I'll show you cats funny." He swiped at a huge brown tabby tom. The tom whirled around and snapped at the bumblebee-striped cat.

"What's your name, Grumpy?" The brown tabby growled. The tom shrank down.

"Axel. My nickname is Stinger," the striped tom replied, his voice now sounding scared.

Well, he's really gotten himself into a heck of a lot of trouble. Hurricane thought. *I hope they don't go so far as getting Fletch.*

Fletch was the leader of the club. He created it. Some cats could sign up for a job as a Guard, which was pretty much like the club's police force. There was also the job as the club's watch-cat, the one who kept an eye on the door in case humans intruded. Though the job could be quite boring, every now and then, the watch-cat could be a huge hero. Finally, there was the co-leader, the cat that helped out Fletch in leading the club. Tazer was the co-leader. Otherwise, if you're not leader, a Guard, a watch-cat, or co-leader, you're simply a club member. But club members are required to earn their keep in the club by hunting for it.

"I'm guessing your nickname comes from looking like a bumblebee and having a bad temper, correct?" the brown tabby tom commented.

Stinger hissed and arched his back, making the jet-black stripes along his spine glint in the lantern light. "Who are you callin' a bumblebee? And I do *not* have a bad temper, thank you very much!"

The huge dark brown tabby tom struck out a paw, knocking Stinger off his feet. "You really need to take a look in the mirror, Bumblebee," the dark brown tabby joked. His companions looked anxiously at each other. The tom pinned Stinger down with a huge paw. "Want to know my name? It's Thorn. You know why?" The tabby hissed. Stinger shook his head. "Because of my claws." He slid out one thorn-sharp claw from the paw pinning Stinger down. Stinger winced. Thorn then slid out all the claws from his free front paw and showed them to Stinger.

"Here's the proof, Bumblebee," Thorn hissed, a grin seeping across his face.

The whole room went silent. Thorn raised his free paw high above his head, positioning it at an angle so that if he brought it down, it would be brought down on Stinger.

"Hurricane!" A sweet voice rang in Hurricane's ear. He turned to see Lexie's terrified face. "I can't take much more of this! Can we *please* leave for a while? Like, to hunt or something?"

"Are you kidding? This is better than TV," Hurricane meowed. *All this over some talking?* He took a bite of his mouse. A hurt look seemed to appear on Lexie's face.

"Alright, alright. But seriously, it was just getting good!" Hurricane led the way out the entrance, Lexie hard on his tail. Jax and Link stopped the two.

"And just where do you think you're going at this time of night?" Link meowed. "It's almost 11:30! Stay in the shelter of the club's fort."

"Excuse me Link, but Lexie and I are going hunting," Hurricane stated with fake politeness.

"There's plenty of food inside," Jax pointed out. "We can go without more food until morning."

"Look, if we promise to go through the whole identification ordeal when we get back, *then* will you let us hunt?" Hurricane asked, annoyed.

Link and Jax looked at each other for a moment, then Jax leaned over and whispered something into Link's ear. Link's whiskers twitched with approval, and then he turned his gaze back to Hurricane and Lexie.

"Without any arguments?" Link asked hopefully. "Or eye rolling? Or any exasperated sighing?"

"Whatever you say, Your Majesty," Hurricane growled.

"For once, we'll actually be able to go through the identification process without any drama!" Jax mewed happily.

"Why do you take such delight in making cats go through it, anyway?" Lexie asked.

"Oh, it's just fun to annoy them, that's all."

Chapter 7

"Well, that was…"

"Odd?"

"Yeah."

Hurricane and Lexie were now padding along the sidewalk. They knew it wasn't the best idea for stray cats to walk along a busy New York street, out there in the open, but they didn't really care.

"Now what?" Lexie asked. The bright lights of the New York City street made her blue eyes twinkle, and illuminated her whitish-yellow pelt. They also made her thin orange and black tabby stripes glint.

Wow.

"You almost look silver," Lexie commented, looking over Hurricanes jet-black pelt.

"Really?" Hurricane asked. He turned his head around to look at his fur. Lexie was right; his fur looked silver. "Cool."

That was when they heard it. Barking. Loud, angry barking. The two whipped around to see a pack of dogs hurtling toward them, quite a ways down the sidewalk, but getting closer with each stride.

That's not Shade! Hurricane thought in panic. He took a closer look. He recognized the lead dog from somewhere. *Dark gray and dark brown patches… pointy ears, one flops over halfway… short fur… long tail… huge paws… long snout… that's… that's… Snag! Snag and his group of stray dogs! The one's that always bully Shade!*

Hurricane whirled round to face Lexie. She was staring at the approaching six-dog-pack, Snag and his five followers. Lexie turned her head to face him.

"Lexie, run."

"What?"

"Run!"

"Aren't you going to follow me?"

27

Hurricane turned to see the dogs closer than ever. They didn't have any time to argue. They had to make a run for it.

"Yes! Fine! Now *go!*" Lexie hissed and the two took off running. Hurricane knew that it would have been better if he had told Lexie to run back to the club and for him to lead the dogs away, but he also knew that Lexie would never have gone for it.

The two ran as fast as their legs could carry them, but Lexie fell back. A dog grabbed her tail, and pulled her toward itself. The other dogs continued their pursuit of Hurricane.

"Lexie!" Hurricane yowled. Hurricane didn't know what to do. He couldn't leave his best friend behind, but he couldn't stop running either.

He took a leap of faith.

Hurricane spun around as fast as friction would allow. He knew it was stupid, but he had to jump on the dogs' *backs.* He thought of going through their legs, but there were possibilities that wouldn't work. The dogs might close their legs and barricade the way out. They would then be able to reach down and grab him.

Hurricane knew that the dogs would grab at him no matter what. There were downfalls and upsides to that as well. The downfall would be that one of them actually did catch him and bring him down. The upside was, if he was fast enough, a dog would grab at him and he'd leap out of the way. The dog, instead of catching him, would fall onto the dog that Hurricane was just leaping off of. The two dogs would trip, therefore falling and getting tangled in a heap. That would give Hurricane more time get away.

Hurricane made a huge bound above Snag. The mutt snapped at Hurricane while he was still in mid-leap. He missed him by an inch. Hurricane landed right on Snag's broad back. He stood there for a split second, allowing the dog behind Snag to snap at him. Just as the dog was bringing its fangs down on Hurricane, he leaped away. The dog toppled down on top of Snag, and the two fell to the sidewalk. He did the same thing to the next two. He had just *leaped over* four dogs!

There was one left. The two stood in front of each other, hissing and growling. Hurricane made the first move. He swiped at the dog, scoring its fur. The dog yelped in pain, giving Hurricane time to speed around it.

Hurricane saw Lexie and the sixth dog tussling. Lexie spat and hissed while the dog growled and barked. Hurricane let out a yowl, and sprang at the dog's face. The dog yelped, then shook Hurricane off its face, giving Lexie time to spring out of the canine's grasp. The two cats dashed away from the fighting scene. But all the dogs were on the sidewalk. No alleys were nearby; all of the buildings were connected. The two veered off into the busy street. They barely missed being hit by a taxi.

That's when the van came out of nowhere. It's engine roared, striking fear into Hurricane's heart, and a spasm of terror sliced through him.

The headlights of the car dazzled the cats for a moment. The whole world seemed to go silent. Everything went in slow motion. Hurricane suddenly thought about Everest's words, the prophecy that a cat and wolf-dog would save the world from everlasting darkness, and that they were those two prophesized cat and dog. He thought of Shade and Eco. Of Earth and Everest. Of Lexie, Fletch and Tazer. Of Link and Jax. He even thought of the rude cat, Stinger. Even of the huge dark brown tabby tomcat, Thorn. *Even* of the white she-cat. He was brought back to the storm, to the abandoned house, the field with the grove of trees to the east. To the clearing inside of the grove of trees where the huge pointed boulder was positioned in the middle. To the storage room for the club. The car revved nearer by the second. He was going to die…

Hurricane was suddenly brought back to consciousness. Blasting noises of New York City hit him like a sledgehammer. The car's headlights blinded him.

"Lexie! Get down!" Hurricane yowled. She wouldn't budge. He was sure that she was in her own flashback, just as he was a second ago. Her eyes were as wide as moons, her mouth hanging open in a silent screech. Her eyes were reflecting the bright headlights.

Hurricane sprang at Lexie, knocking her to the ground. She screamed in shock. The car roared over them. The pavement was cold from the night chill. It had to be at least 12:30 a.m. Two more cars sped above them. Finally, when there was a pause in that lane, the two sprang to their feet and hurtled themselves toward the sidewalk. They rested when their paws met the concrete.

"Oh… my God…" Hurricane forced out between pants.

"That… was close… we were almost-," Lexie coughed. "Killed!"

"I know," panted Hurricane. "I know."

The two caught their breath and lapped up water from a nearby puddle. "We could have died. But, we- we survived."

A chill ran up Hurricane's spine as he imagined the huge black tires of the car crushing him under their weight. "Yeah." He lapped up more water, avoiding further conversation on the horrifying topic. "Let's go."

Lexie flicked an ear. They swiveled all around. "You hear that?" she asked.

Hurricane listened. *Paws. Huge paws. I think about four to six dogs... No! Not again!*

Hurricane knew Snag and his group when he heard them.

"Run!"

The two ran for dear life. They weren't going through another fight.

Soon the dogs came into sight.

"You're not getting away *that* easily, cats!" Snag barked.

"Run! Run! Ru-," Hurricane ran into something and was knocked to the ground. He looked up to see a familiar gray and black face looking down at him in amazement. A green pouch hung from the face's neck.

"Hurricane?"

"Shade!"

"Dog!" Lexie screeched. "Run, Hurricane! It's a dog!"

"Don't worry Lexie, this is my good friend, Shade."

"What? But he's a *dog*! We almost just got *killed* by a pack of dogs!"

Shade and Hurricane exchanged a glance.

"Lexie, run back to the club as fast as you can. I need to talk to Shade."

"What? I'm not leaving my best friend alone with a dog!"

"Come into this alley you two. Snag's group is almost here." The two cats followed Shade into the nearby alley. They waited behind a trashcan as Snag's group sped past.

"Wow. That was close," Hurricane panted.

"Phew," Shade sighed. He turned his gaze to Lexie. "Hey, wait a sec, I remember you! You were with Hurricane when you two got under my paws. That was the first time that I ever saw Hurricane."

"So that dog was you!" Lexie exclaimed. "What were you thinking, standing in the middle of the alley like an idiot?"

"Why were you two cats in such a hurry that day?" Shade asked, acting as though Lexie had never said anything.

"We were getting away from two human kids that thought we looked 'cute'. Now, Lexie *please* go back to the club. I absolutely *have* to talk to Shade."

"Fine!" Lexie spat. She spun around and ran back to the alley.

"Tell Link and Jax that I'm still hunting!" Hurricane yowled after her.

All she did was flatten her ears and kept on running.

"Who's *she*?" Shade asked.

"Just an old friend," Hurricane replied. "Her name's Lexie. Sometimes I call her Lex for short."

"Okay. Look, I've been thinking."

"Well, congrats. That doesn't happen very often," Hurricane joked.

The two laughed for a moment. "Rude." Shade shoved the cat playfully.

"Anyways, I was just thinking… What do we do about that… er… evil darkness? Just forget about it and wait for Everest to turn up somewhere? Or go back to the abandoned house and see if he's there?"

31

"You have a point, but..."

"Come on. Let's go back. I mean, imagine what will happen if we don't. The Earth will be submerged in darkness. And dude, seriously, I'm afraid of the dark."

The two laughed again.

Hurricane took a look down the alley where Lexie had disappeared. He sighed. Shade was right; they had to go back. A pleading look was on Shade's face.

"Alright, let's go."

Chapter 8

Once the two came back upon the abandoned house where they had first encountered Everest, they stopped. Something felt... different.

"Do you feel that?" Shade asked.

"Yeah, it almost feels... cold. Or, no, not cold, but... um, I don't know how to explain it."

"I know what you mean," Shade commented. "But it's the middle of November. Isn't it normal to be cold?"

"But it's not really cold," Hurricane observed. He shivered. Something didn't feel right. "It's almost like that feeling you get when a ghost passes by. Except it's a lot more... unsettling."

"Instincts!" Shade exclaimed.

"What?" Hurricane asked, bewildered. *Is he okay?*

"It's our instincts. They're telling us that something's not safe about this place." Shade sniffed the wind. "But it also feels like how you described it. Like a ghost passing by, yet, quite a bit more, well, unsettling."

"I say we go back." Hurricane turned around to walk back across the street. This place felt a lot spookier than the first time that they came here to collect the Earth Element.

"Oh no you don't." Shade turned and grabbed Hurricane by the tail.

"Ouch!" Hurricane yowled. He whipped around and clouted Shade on the snout with a hiss.

"Ow!" Shade barked, covering his nose with a paw.

"*Never* grab a cat's tail!" Hurricane hissed.

"Never *smack* a dog's *snout!*" Shade growled.

Hurricane arched his back. The fur along it bristled. He admitted to himself that no matter what, they would have to go inside at some point. "Come on."

The two walked through the permanently ajar door. It had fallen off its hinges, and was now propped at an angle in the doorway. Years of weather and rain had made it sink into the soil and become stuck in the ground.

"I've never liked this place," Hurricane commented while looking at a cracked window.

"Me neither," said Shade.

Once the two were inside, they took a quick glance in the direction where Everest had come from the first time that they were there.

No one was there.

"That's odd," woofed Shade. "I remember: You were upstairs. I had stopped on that rug over there," Shade pointed with his snout toward a faded oval-shaped rug. "I was facing the couch, and Everest came from the kitchen, which I had been facing away from."

"Did you say anything?" Hurricane asked.

"Say anything?" Shade echoed.

"For instance, something like, 'Ooh, this is spooky' or 'Hello' or something."

"Um... I think so."

"Then I have an idea."

Chapter 9

Shade stood on the faded rug while facing the couch, just as he had done the first time that they were there. Hurricane had gone upstairs to the same bedroom and spot. Shade took a moment to remember what he had said. He was ready.

"Ready down there?" he heard Hurricane mew from upstairs.

Shade gulped. He wasn't sure how he felt about meeting Everest again. "Ready."

Hurricane counted down to when they would reenact the scene. "Three… two… one… go!"

Hurricane heard Shade clear his throat. *This had better work.*

"Hello? Is anybody here?"

Silence.

Shade tried again. "*Hello*? Is anybody here?"

Still nothing.

"Are you sure you're saying the exact same thing?" Hurricane meowed.

"I'm sure!" Shade barked back.

Well, if he is *saying what he said the last time, then this plan isn't working.*

Hurricane hopped back down the stairs.

"Okay, new plan," Hurricane demanded.

They both stared blankly at each other.

"Well? Got anything?"

"Nope," Shade answered. "You?"

"Nope," Hurricane meowed sadly.

"You two always try too hard."

Hurricane and Shade whirled around in the direction of the voice.

A grinning face with an eye-patch met their eyes.

Chapter 10

"Everest, where have you been?" They both asked over and over.

Everest let out a hearty laugh. "Just over in the Rockies. It's almost the Winter Solstice, you know."

"That must be very exciting for all the Sighter Dogs, I'd guess," Shade observed.

"Yes, yes," Everest replied. "All of us Sighters are very good friends. We're always excited for the Rocky Mountain Sighter Meeting."

"That's the name of it?" Hurricane asked.

"Why, no. It goes by many names. The Rocky Sighter Dog News Exchange, the Meeting of the Sighter Dogs, the Rocky Mountain Sighter Dog Meeting, and some young Sighters that are still in training tend to call it the Sighter Festival. But the name that was first thought of by the first Sighters was the Rocky Mountain Sighter Dog Meeting.

"The Sighter Festival? Why a festival?" They both asked.

"Oh, it's not just a news exchange meeting. There are activities before and after the annual news exchange. There's even a reenactment play by the Sighters still in training, called students, of how the Sighters came to be. It really is quite a fun jubilee."

"Wait, so you train puppies to be Sighters?" Shade asked.

"Precisely."

"Do they sign up?"

"No, because the Sighters are unknown to the rest of the world. Well, with an exception of you two and a few lucky animals who have discovered us. But they are all forced to swear not to tell a soul of our existence."

"So, how do pups become Sighters?" asked Hurricane. "And you said that there were Sighter cats as well!"

"Pups are born into the life of a Sighter. They are born from other Sighters, and train as their parents did. Also, each pup is given a red and a blue feather to wear behind their ear when they start training. It's a custom." Everest turned his head sideways to show them his own two feathers.

"Now, about the Sighter Cats," Hurricane demanded.

"Almost exactly the same. Prophesies, students, a meeting on the Winter Solstice. The only real difference is that they're cats, they're named for constellations, and they meet in a place unknown to the Sighter Dogs."

"Do you ever meet up with them?" Hurricane asked.

"Rarely. Only for drastic measures, like now, with this overpowering darkness. They will be meeting us at the Rocky Mountain Sighter Meeting."

"Okay, okay. Look Everest, we came here to learn of the second element. We need to know!" Shade began to pace.

"Don't want to chat? We have time you know."

"We do?" they asked in unison.

"Yes, but I can see that you two would like to get on with the mission. The next element is Air. Well, off you go."

"Wait!" They both yelled at once.

Too late. A white flash obscured the living room, and soon the two were lost in a swirl of light.

Chapter 11

Before either of them could say a word, they were swept to a rocky, barren landscape. Jagged rocks pointed up out of the ground, some a few feet taller than Shade. A thick fog covered everything more than three yards ahead of the two. Strong wind buffeted their fur.

"Air... the second element," a voice whispered in their ears.

"Come on, let's go" said Hurricane.

"Let's go... where?" asked Shade. "We need a guide."

"Your wish is my command!"

"Who's that?" yelped Shade, spinning around.

"Only me!" yipped a puppy voice. Shade looked down and Hurricane turned around.

Standing there was a German Shepherd puppy.

"Why do the Sighters keep getting baby animals as our guides?" Hurricane asked, scowling.

"I'm Titus! I'm going to take you to the Air Element! Follow *me!*" Titus began to scamper off into the fog.

"Wait up!" Hurricane and Shade both said.

"You see? *This* is why I don't like having kittens and puppies as our guides. They're way too quick to get to the point. Way too excited. He didn't even give us the Air Pouch."

"I think that someone needs to take a look in the mirror," Shade countered with a look.

"Who, me? No way! I'm nothing like that!" Hurricane argued.

"Keep up you two!" they heard Titus yip.

Shade looked at Hurricane.

"Okay, okay. Fine. I'm pretty pushy too," Hurricane admitted.

Shade grinned. The two kept following Titus.

"Hey, Titus," Hurricane meowed.

"Yep! What?" Titus yipped back.

"You know where we're going, right?

"Well, duh!" Titus laughed.

"Then where?" Hurricane wondered.

"To the big rock that curves up out of the ground!"

"What?" Hurricane bewilderedly asked.

"One end of the rock sticks *high* out of the ground. It curves at the top, then comes back down at the other end and touches the ground again. It looks like a great big half loop! The element will be levitating underneath the curve at the top, in-between the two pillar-rocks that stick out of the ground."

"Um… okay?" Shade replied.

The three walked for a while longer.

Hurricane became annoyed. "My paws are sore! Are we almost there?"

"Be patient," Shade ordered.

"Nearly!" Titus replied. "We should be seeing it right about… now!"

Hurricane bumped into a rock just as the fog dispersed.

"Ouch! What the…?"

"Ta-da!" Titus squeaked.

Shade and Hurricane looked up. Titus had been correct. It was a big boulder that looked like a half loop.

Hurricane rubbed his head. "Did it have to turn up so suddenly?"

"Hey wait, I've seen a rock formation like this!" Shade realized. "Like in the cowboy movies. Out in the desert there are all those rocks in shapes, right?"

"Right...?" Hurricane answered.

"Well, this is one that turns up a lot!"

Hurricane looked up at the rock formation. "Oh! Now I remember. Yeah, you see these in deserts."

"Look you two!" Titus barked suddenly.

The fog around the inside of the formation cleared. Floating in its place was a white hollow ball. The inside of it was empty.

"Hey! It looks like a bubble!" Titus yelped excitedly.

"It's just like the globe that held the Earth Element!" Shade woofed. "Except, it's white, and there's nothing in it."

"Wait a sec!" Titus seemed to suddenly realize something. "I almost forgot!" He disappeared around to the other side of the rock formation. When he came back, he was holding a small white pouch with a white ribbon going through it. A silver capital "A" was embroidered on the pouch.

"Oh yeah. The ever important Air Pouch," Hurricane observed. "But it doesn't look like we'll be using it. We don't have anything to put inside it."

"Of course you do," a strange voice said.

Hurricane and Shade didn't even jump that time. Turning around, their eyes met a white she-cat with wings and silver swirl marks patterning her fur.

"I am Air," the winged cat began, "keeper of the second element. I have guarded it awaiting your arrival. Titus, come here."

"Okay, Air!" Titus yelped. He scampered over and sat down next to Air.

"Hello, Air," Shade and Hurricane both said simultaneously.

41

Air turned her gaze over to Shade and Hurricane. "I understand that Earth already explained to you how to collect the elements, yes?"

"Oh yes," Shade replied. "She did. But, what, exactly are we collecting?"

"The second element, silly!" Titus pointed out.

"Oh, Titus." Air turned to the German Shepherd puppy. "You crack me up." She turned back to Hurricane and Shade. "Air, of course. I understand that it seems odd, but it isn't as though there is nothing in that globe. Air is a form of matter as well. It is made up of molecules and atoms like any other solid, liquid, plasma, or non-Newtonian-liquid."

"Plasma?" Hurricane asked.

"Yes. Plasma is the fourth form of matter. Most only know there to be three, but there are scientifically five. Plasma is actually what fire is made up of."

"What on Earth is non-Newtonian-liquid?" Shade questioned.

"Things like ketchup and hair-gel. Pretty much just goop." Air smiled on the last sentence.

"So, anyway, how *do* we collect the Air Element? It's not like we can put it in the pouch."

"Of course you can. That pouch is a special one. It acts like a vacuum. But the only thing that it will suck in is this specific air in this globe." Air pointed with an outstretched paw to the globe. "Now, do as Earth taught you. Collect the air."

Shade looked at Hurricane. "May I this time?"

Hurricane sighed. "Fine," he huffed.

"Well Hurricane, that means that *you* get to wear the Air Pouch," Air mewed.

"How do you know my... oh, never mind," Hurricane meowed as Titus tied the ribbon that held the pouch around Hurricane's neck.

Shade grabbed at the globe holding the air. "So I'm guessing I look at it and say, 'Air, the second element' to make it stop floating, right?" Shade asked, balancing on his back paws and looking at Air.

"Correct."

"Okay," Shade answered. He turned his face to the levitating globe. "Air, the-"

A loud cawing cut him off.

"What was that?" Hurricane asked, the Air Pouch dangling from his neck.

"Yeah? What *was* that?" Shade repeated.

Air's ears swiveled. Her tail-tip twitched. Suddenly she unfolded her wings and stuck them high in the foggy air. Her claws slid out and scraped against the completely rock-covered ground, making an ear piercing *screech* noise, like nails on a chalkboard.

"Everyone get down!" She yowled. The echo of her voice rang all around them, accompanied by a strong flapping noise somewhere above the two cats and two dogs.

"What?" Hurricane meowed loudly. "Why?"

"Just get dow-" Air's yowl was quickly lost in a much louder cawing and a mad flapping. A black blob appeared in the fog above them, becoming larger, meaning *closer*, with each passing moment.

The biggest raven that any of them had ever seen appeared out of the vast gray, it's razor sharp talons bearing down on the group.

"*Run!*" Air screeched.

Chapter 12

Hurricane fled for the cover of the rocks. Instincts told him to flee the premises completely, but he knew that wasn't an option. The fog was far too thick, the raven would surely find him, and he knew that if he did leave the element and the journey, the prophecy would be shattered and the Earth consumed by a sickening black darkness. No, it was his duty to the world to stand his ground and protect the Air Element with all his strength, and be willing to give his life for the cause.

It was his duty to his friends.

To the club in which he lived.

To the prophecy.

To the world.

His duty as a cat.

And as a *soldier*, even.

Yes, he and Shade were truly soldiers.

Hurricane perched at the top of a rock pile thinking these thoughts. They all went through his mind in the moment that he was standing up there. He realized that if he did hide behind there now, his duty would not be complete.

I can't hide behind there like a coward.

Hurricane leaped from his perch on the rock pile. He had originally climbed up to the top of the small heap to then jump back down to the other side and hide. But he knew that they couldn't just leave Air to fend off the raven all by herself.

He leaped up into the fog. For a split second his claws scraped feathers. Ghastly, disgusting, black, oily feathers. He soared like an eagle for a few heavenly moments, taking in a small feeling of freedom and rest in those gray clouds before literally falling into battle.

"You two have an amazing destiny before you," Everest had said. *I remember. I remember. I remember…*

Hurricane suddenly felt himself falling. His paws touched cold hard rock. He looked up to see a huge black shadow through the fog. It flapped its wings, sometimes lifting up off the ground to slash out with its long, curled talons.

The fog began to clear as Hurricane sprang forward. He saw Air cornered against a boulder, lips peeled back in a menacing hiss and her ears flattened against her head. Her tail lashed back and forth, her back was arched with the fur bristling. She lashed out again and again at the raven, claws sharp and unsheathed. Her wings pointed straight up in the air, ready to lift off the ground and fight while flying if she had to.

This seemingly calm, wise and beautiful cat looked dangerous.

The raven was cornering her. This was the biggest bird Hurricane had ever seen, and not only did it intend to kill them, Hurricane was actually going to fight it.

"Hurricane! Help! Make it go away!" Hurricane heard the voice from somewhere among the boulders behind the rock formation where the Air Element was still levitating. He suddenly saw the brown and black face, more scared than anything.

"Don't worry Titus!" Hurricane yowled. "Just stay down!"

Hurricane turned his head to the bird. He concentrated.

He crouched.

He was ready.

He leaped, claws outstretched.

"You cannot have us!" He screeched.

The raven whirled around snapping at Hurricane. Hurricane grabbed the raven's neck with his claws and held on tight. The bird lifted off the ground, Hurricane being dragged along with it. The black tom stretched his back claws to the ground and clung on to a few curved rocks sticking up. The raven flapped harder. And harder.

"Shade!" Hurricane yowled out to the rocks. "I need backup!"

His hind claws gave way. He was abruptly lifted up into the fog.

"No!" He heard a cat yowl. He suddenly saw Air pushing off the ground and flapping her wings strongly. Her ears flat against her head, claws outstretched, she gave a mighty flap with her wings that sent her soaring forward. "You cannot take him! He has a prophecy to fulfill!"

Hurricane scraped his claws down the raven's oily neck. It let out an ear splitting screech, and the young tomcat fell off its back. Air fought it back down to the ground, revealing a fresh set of scars on her silver and white pelt. Hurricane sprang at its beak, making it let out a loud caw. "Shade! We need you right now! It's impossible to fight it off with only two cats! We need more than two sets of claws! We need a wolf right now!"

Suddenly a black and gray shape seemed to soar through the fog. It landed on the ground with a thump, revealing itself to be Shade. He threw himself at the raven, pinning it to the ground. He clamped down hard on the wing with his fangs, making the raven cry out.

Hurricane's jaw dropped for a moment before springing at the face of the raven.

Hurricane quickly turned to Shade. "Thanks," he panted, before making four long claw marks down the raven's chest. It squealed in pain.

The raven tore itself from Shade's fangs, leaving behind a swirling pile of black feathers. Shade reared up as the raven lashed out with its talons. It caught him in the leg, leaving three long gashes. Shade howled in pain.

Suddenly a small brown and black shape leaped onto the raven's back, sinking its fangs into the back.

It was Titus.

"Titus, no!" Air yowled. "You can't take him on! He will destroy you! That raven! He will kill you!"

Titus didn't listen; his fangs sank deeper into the back.

The raven screeched, then lifted off the ground. It began to disappear into the fog, with Titus riding it.

"No!" all three yelled.

Air turned to Hurricane. "Grab my paw! Quickly!" she pressed her paw to his. Hurricane hesitated. The moment Air's paw touched his, a blast of courage seared through him. Her magic was giving him strength.

He stood there, relishing the bravery that was overwhelming him. He felt as though he could fight *ten* ravens if he was put up to it.

"Hurricane! Stop daydreaming! Grab. My. Paw!" Air was yelling even louder now. Hurricane returned to their predicament, leaving his world of daydreaming about fighting off more ravens than ever before.

The courage still pumped through his veins. He could barely feel his bleeding gashes now. With a quick glance at the Air Pouch bound around his neck, he clasped onto Air's paw. "Shade!" he yowled. "Protect the Air Element! We have to save Titus!"

"I will!" Shade barked back.

Air suddenly began flapping her white-feathered wings. She lifted off the ground, Hurricane being pulled along as well.

"We're flying!" Hurricane meowed excitedly.

"No, I'm flying," Air pointed out. "You're just being dragged along."

Hurricane looked at her, annoyed. Her eyes were glued on the fog in front of them, trying to make out the shape of the raven's body.

"Here's the plan!" She began. "I will fly above the raven, and then you let go and fall onto its back."

"Are you crazy?" he yowled.

"It's the only way!" she answered. "You must weaken the bird, then grab Titus! I will then battle the bird back down to the ground! But you must jump off before the bird touches the ground, in the case that it is a trick and he is not really landing!"

"Titus and I'll both injure ourselves!"

"You must! Hurricane, I have wings! I understand how birds fly!"

Hurricane hesitated, and then nodded. "Alright. Hey! I thought I saw something!"

"I did too!" Air answered.

A blurry black shape appeared through the fog. A spatter of brown colored its back.

"The raven and Titus!" Air yowled. "We must lift higher than they are, so that you can dive!"

Air flew higher into the fog. When the two of them knew that they were at a higher altitude than the raven, Air pressed forward, trying to get directly above the bird.

"We're as accurate as possible!" Air mewed. "I will fly a bit to one side of the raven instead of being directly above him. If we are directly above and you drop, you will miss the raven completely. But then it's up to you!"

Hurricane took a deep breath as Air positioned to the right side of the raven, positioning Hurricane directly above. If he fell short, or made a wrong move, he would miss the raven completely. The ground was very far down now.

He breathed deeply. He couldn't miss. He let go of Air's soft paw.

Hurricane turned his body at a vertical angle. He stretched out his paws far in front of him, claws unsheathed. He felt like a skydiver. The raven came closer with each passing second. It's black feathered back acted like a landing pad for the young tom. He imagined a big red target on the raven's back. Hurricane imagined wearing goggles and a pack with a parachute inside. He pretended that Titus was simply a landing instructor instead of a captured victim. He could almost see pup with a med-kit and two yellow flags in his paws.

Hurricane smiled.

Titus hadn't even noticed the two cats coming to save him. His scared little face was pointed directly ahead, in the same direction as the raven's. The raven hadn't noticed them either. It kept on flapping its huge wings, intent on its task to take Titus away to a nest or other location.

"Titus, look out!" Hurricane yowled as he began to land on the imaginary target. Titus whipped around in time to see Hurricane diving down. He jumped further towards the raven's head. Just as the raven began to turn to see the flying tomcat, Hurricane landed, scoring his claws along the raven's right wing.

"Bite its left wing! Now!" Hurricane ordered. Titus did as he was told, and sank his teeth into the left wing. Hurricane clawed at the right one. The raven screeched. Unable to bare the pain any longer, it began to dive. That's when Air sliced through the fog.

"You will not destroy us!" she yowled at it. Air grabbed the wing of the raven and dragged it downwards. Once they were a short distance from the ground, Air called out. "Drop, now! Go! Go! Go!"

Hurricane gave Titus a shove. "Jump! Before the raven lifts off again!"

Titus revealed to Hurricane a terrified expression. "No! I can't!"

"You can! Now go!"

Titus took one last look at the ground, and then nodded to Hurricane. He spun around, and then jumped.

Hurricane was ready. But when he began to leap off the raven's back, he got caught on something. He turned around to see what it was.

The ribbon going through the Air Pouch had gotten caught on the raven's wing.

No!

Hurricane started madly pulling at the ribbon. It wasn't coming loose. He tried untying it.

"Hurricane!" He heard Air call. "Jump, now! The raven is lifting off again!"

Hurricane panicked. The ribbon wouldn't untie, and the raven was beginning to fly.

"Air!" Hurricane yowled. "The ribbon on the pouch! It's stuck!"

Air dived toward Hurricane. Quickly and cleanly, she snapped through the ribbon with her teeth. "Come on!" She mewed.

Hurricane leaped off the raven just as it disappeared through the fog.

Air stared at the fog above them. "The Dark Forces are rising. We must act quickly."

"Dark Forces?" Shade echoed.

"Yes. That raven was part of the everlasting darkness Everest explained to you about. The darkness has begun. They are creating an army of Dark Forces. If we do not stop them, they will destroy all of our happiness and light and love. They will engulf the Earth in shadow, and turn every heart black as night. They will rule everything."

"Oh my God," Hurricane breathed.

"Yes. The four elements are our only shield against it. You two are the only ones capable of collecting them."

"Why can't anyone else but us?" Hurricane asked.

"Because you are the only ones that can bear the power. The elements are very strong. You don't know it because you are immune to the strength. But if just anyone tried to touch one of these elements, they would be weakened beyond belief. Only you two can carry them to the outside world."

"The outside world?" Hurricane asked, cringing from a gash in his shoulder.

Air nodded. "You are in a magical place. Here, the elements can be weathered. But in the outside world, like New York, the elements would destroy everything. Their power would be far too overwhelming. But if either of you are carrying them, that will not happen. For instance, pretend that some puppy was accidentally sent to go get the Water Element. Once he brought it back to wherever he lived, since he is not one of the chosen, the element would overpower the world and destroy it from the inside. But if either of you are carrying it in the outside world, being the chosen ones, the element would not harm the planet. You are the only ones capable."

Shade looked down at the Earth Pouch around his neck holding the Earth Element. He suddenly felt like he was carrying a deadly weapon.

"Alright Shade," Hurricane meowed. "Grab that element."

Chapter 13

"Air, the second element," Shade slowly said.

White lights exploded from the floating globe. It fell into Shade's black paws. He turned to Air.

Shade tilted his head. Air nodded. Shade pressed on both ends of the globe, and it disappeared. In his hands lay a white shining sphere. He looked at Air. "This is the Air Element?"

Air nodded again. "Yes. It is circled by a white shining cover so that it can be seen."

"Wait," Hurricane meowed.

Air looked towards him. "Yes?"

"The pouch's ribbon. You cut it, remember?"

Air simply walked up to Hurricane and took the pouch in her paws. She clasped her paws together around the pouch, and then covered her arms completely with her wings. She closed her eyes, and with a flash of white light, opened her wings once more. She then opened her clasped paws and put down the pouch in front of Hurricane.

The ribbon was good as new.

Titus hopped over and retied it around Hurricane's neck

Hurricane walked up to Shade, the Air Pouch wide open. "Drop it in," he instructed.

Shade allowed the second element to fall from his paws into the Air Pouch. The silver embroidered "A" turned gold.

"Well done, both of you."

Hurricane and Shade turned to see Everest sitting beside Air. "Yes, very well done," Air echoed. "You fought that raven well, Hurricane. I was glad to have you as a battle partner," she added to the young tomcat.

Hurricane blushed.

51

"You did good as well, Shade. You jumped onto the raven with great strength and force."

"Thank you," he answered modestly.

"You two have earned yourselves a very smooth ride home. But remember that there are two more elements to collect." With a last wink from his good eye, Everest disappeared.

"Thank you both. I really appreciate your help." Air touched noses to both of them.

"Thank you so much, Hurricane. You truly are a soldier," she whispered with her nose pressed against his, before a flash of light tore him from her light touch.

Chapter 14

Hurricane and Shade were whisked back to the abandoned house. They were both standing on the faded oval rug.

Hurricane felt warm.

Shade turned to the tom. "What an adventure! Did you see me jump on that raven? I don't know what came over me but... wow! That was great!

"You should have seen me skydiving onto its back *while* it was *flying*. It was crazy! I let go of Air's paw and literally fell onto it! I was riding a raven! I'm going to tell Lexie all about it!"

Shade's face fell. "I don't think that's a good idea."

"What? Why?"

"Because, if we tell others about the darkness, they'll tell their friends, and everyone will panic," Shade stated solemnly.

Hurricane had to admit that Shade had a point.

"And, Lexie might try to follow us next time if you tell her. Remember what Air said about animals that haven't been chosen touching the elements? She could seriously get hurt."

"You're right. I won't tell her or anyone. You won't either, right?"

"Right. Okay, let's both head back home," said Shade.

As the two of them walked outside, they looked up. It was as dark as it was when they first went in the abandoned house, and the moon was in the same spot.

"I don't think that any time passed while we were gone," Hurricane pointed out.

"Yeah. It's like we never left."

They both looked at each other. "Whoa," they said in unison.

"Well, bye Shade."

"Bye Hurricane."

The two walked in opposite directions down the sidewalk.

I wonder what the club will think of my pouch.

Hurricane decided to hunt as a way to hide his tracks. He caught a squirrel and two mice. He even fished around in the dumpster and found a perfectly good, unopened loaf of bread. Then he found a half eaten bag of chips.

Wow. Pretty lucky.

Hurricane put the mice and squirrel in the chip bag. He dragged the bread loaf and bag with him. He had to walk backwards.

When he finally got back, Link and Jax, the two Entrance Guards, stopped him.

"Halt. What is your-" Link began.

"My name is Hurricane. I am four years old. I am a black tomcat. I live in the Fletch Cat Club. Your names are Jax and Link, and I have been hunting. Oh, the password is, 'no club cat fears the night'. Happy?"

Link and Jax stared at him for a moment, and then Link motioned towards the crack in the wall with his paw to allow entry. Hurricane smiled and walked in.

"Wait. Come back out here," Link ordered.

Hurricane gulped. *They saw my pouch!*

Hurricane came back out, dragging the food. "Yes?"

"What's in those bags?" Link asked.

"Chips are in the chips bag of course, and I also caught a squirrel and two mice then put them in it as well. That over there is a perfectly good unopened loaf of bread."

Link grunted. "Jax, check Hurricane's items." Link pointed to the Air Pouch with his nose. "What's that? A holster you can wear on your neck? Looks pretty decorated. Have you got trading items in there? You know that Fletch only allows trades if they've been authorized by him!"

Hurricane gulped. He looked at the pouch. The embroidered letter was still gold which meant the Air Element was still in there. If Link touched it, he would either be terribly weakened, or the planet could face certain doom.

Kind of dramatic, really. But still!

"Nothing. It's empty. It's… uh… a little bag to hold things in! Yeah."

"Really. Where'd you get it?" Link demanded.

I can't tell him where I really got it! Either he won't believe me, or he'll panic about the darkness! But I can't say I bought it either. He'll ask whom I bought it from!

"I uh… Oh yeah!"

I have an idea!

"It's an old gift that I got from a friend a long time ago. I was a kitten when I got it. I was playing with some friends, and when I got back to the club it wasn't around my neck. I had lost it. But today, while I was hunting, I found it in a human's garden!"

"It looks new, though," Link pointed out.

"It was in a sealed plastic bag."

"Now tell me why you are covered in scars and gashes that are bleeding all over the ground." Link was skeptical.

Hurricane looked down to see blood spatters on the alley's asphalt.

Oops.

"Dog fight," He answered. At least that was partly true.

Link looked at Hurricane with squinted eyes for a moment, and then hissed. "Fine," he growled. "Go on in."

Hurricane's whiskers twitched. He smiled. "Thanks." He reached around for the food when Link stopped him.

"Wait. Jax isn't done checking it."

Hurricane rolled his eyes.

Jax's head popped out of the chips bag. "He's good."

Link turned to Hurricane. "*Now* you may take your catches inside the club."

Hurricane nodded formally, grabbed the food, and headed inside.

Many surprised faces met him. He wasn't sure if they were looking at his huge catch, or his cuts and gashes. Or perhaps both.

Lexie ran up to him. "What happened to you? Did the dog do that? He did, didn't he! Wait till I get my paws on that stupid canine…"

"Hold up. I met Snag and his group again, that's all. They let me go. That's all that matters. Now please let me put this food in the stock-box so that I can go to sleep."

"You're lying! That dog! His name was… his name was… oh, what was it? Shade! His name was Shade! Shade did this to you!"

"No, he didn't! Besides you, Shade is my best friend. Now *please* let me put this stuff away so that I can get some sleep. Snag and his group really did a number on me, as you can see."

Lexie looked at Hurricane for a moment, then hissed. "Snag's really got some nerve. Look at you; you're bleeding like crazy. Go put that stuff away."

Hurricane turned around, and started to walk to the cardboard box in the corner that held all of the food.

She fell for it. Neither Snag nor Shade did this to me. That stupid raven of the Dark Forces did. But Snag's group did leave a few *cuts when Lexie and I were fighting them.*

Hurricane dropped the food in the stockpile and turned around. A silver tabby spoke to him. "Congrats on the catch, Hurricane. That'll feed us for a while."

"Thanks, Silver," he replied.

56

Hurricane walked back to his spot in the club. He could see Lexie padding towards her bed just before Jasmine's five kittens jumped into it again. He saw them all wailing for Jasmine, and Lexie rolling her eyes before closing them. He laughed to himself. He could see Lexie open one eye and look at him, then mouth the words "good night". He mouthed them back. She closed her eyes once more.

Hurricane limped over to where he slept.

He settled into his flour sack bed, and pulled the towel over himself. His muscles ached, his paws were sore, and his cuts stung. But he was still able to fall deeply into sleep.

Hurricane could still see Air and feel her soft, angelic touch.

Destiny

The Encounter: Volume III

Chapter 15

"Who are they? I want their names! Give me their names!" The Lord of Eternal Darkness banged his huge fist on the wooden table. The Dark Council sat in rows with wine in their goblets and meat on their plates. The Dark Lord sat at the head of the long rectangular table. "I *demand* their names!" He roared once more.

The Dark Lord was the most merciless of all darkness. He commanded every dark force on the planet. He was the one who controlled them and decided their fate. He was known to slay anyone in his army of Dark Forces who disagreed with his decisions. He was a huge jet black-colored dragon, with red spines down his back, blood-red claws, red wings, and red horns upon his head. A red arrowhead shaped point was at the tip of his tail. His fangs were so long that they stuck out of his mouth, making him look like a saber tooth tiger.

The Dark Lord's claws wound around his staff. It was a black stick, with a huge red jewel at the tip. The jewel glowed and made his fangs reflect a red light.

"Our great Lord of Darkness, we are trying our best," growled a large black-and-gray colored creature with curled horns and a long nose. "Our scout got a few bits of information. He knows what the two of them look like. I am *sure* that you will be pleased with his knowledge."

"Then bring him in!" the Dark Lord demanded. The two huge metal doors at the other end of the room swung open. The Lord of Eternal Darkness peered down the long table at the three creatures in the doorway. Two were werewolves, and in-between the two, being held by the wings, was a raven. The two werewolves dragged the injured raven down the length of the table. They threw him to the ground at the Dark Lord's feet.

The Dark Lord grunted and kicked the exhausted raven further away from him. The raven screeched in pain from his wounds. Claw marks down his neck and back stung like fire. Fangs sinking into them had damaged his wings. They ached horribly, and the Dark Lord kicking at him had done them no better. The Dark Lord's feet were leaving bloody prints where the raven lay on the floor.

The Dark Lord leaned his head toward the raven's face. "Speak," he growled.

In the raven's attempt to talk, all that came out was a scratchy moan. A rattled cough shook from deep in his throat. All his wounds still bled, including the ones in his neck. All his desire to move had seeped out of him. He wanted only to lie there, letting his wounds heal, and his aching muscles to be rested.

The Lord of Darkness' nostrils flared, making smoke blow into the air. He raised his lips, showing rows of basketball-sized teeth, each one sharpened to a point. A growl welled up from deep in his throat. He shoved his staff in the raven's face. "Speak, you stupid excuse for a bird!"

The raven looked up at the Dark Lord's face. The huge dragon wanted answers, and he wanted them *now*. The raven moaned, stood up, walked to the wall, and then sat down with his back against it. He let his head hang to one side, and opened his beak to talk.

"A cat..." he began. "And a dog that I-" he coughed, "that I believe is also half wolf." The raven recalled when the black and gray wolf-dog leaped onto him, howling about itself being a wolf.

"Hmm..." the Dark Lord grunted, sitting back down. He turned his head to the two werewolf guards and nodded at them. They nodded back formally, secured their belts that held countless weapons, and left the meeting room. "So they're not sorcerers or monsters with powers? Only a dog and a cat?"

The raven let out a breath. His eyes drooped. "Yes, sir."

"Excellent," the Dark Lord snarled, stroking his staff. His head suddenly turned to the raven. "Anything else that you would like to share?"

The raven's eyes were closed now. His voice came almost in a whisper. "I believe their names are Shade and Hurricane." He drew in a scratchy breath. "But I couldn't really tell which was which."

"Good, yes. You were there when they were collecting the second element, correct? You were ordered to steal it so that they were unable to collect it. Now, I understand that you have it, don't you?" The Dark Lord twirled his staff with his claws. The raven's eyes shot open. He had left before stealing the element because the four cats and dogs were too strong for him to bear.

"Hand it over," the Dark Lord commanded.

The raven closed his eyes, preparing himself to be punished severely. "I'm sorry, sir," he wheezed. "The four of them were too much for me to handle. I do not have the Air Element."

"What!" the Dark Lord roared. He kicked back his chair and flew up into the air. His wings flapped so harshly that everyone who was sitting down had to shield their faces. The Dark Lord's plate and wine glass went flying. "You were ordered to bring me that element! You have failed!"

The raven wanted to fly out of that room. But after flying all the way back to the Castle of Eternal Darkness with injured wings, his wings wouldn't flap correctly. All he could do was lie there, and await his punishment. What would the Dark Lord do to him? He might roast him by blowing a line of fire from his dragon mouth. Or perhaps he would claw him to shreds. He might even make the guards pile on top of him, using all of their weapons on him at once. His eyes remained closed.

"What is your name, bird?" the Lord of Eternal Darkness snarled. He shoved his staff at the raven, pinning him against the wall. The whole room went silent.

The raven knew this was the end. He coughed. "Banshee. My name is Banshee."

"Banshee," the Dark Lord growled. "Banshee." The dragon shoved at Banshee with his staff once more. "You are a disgrace, Banshee." The Dark Lord landed on the wooden floor.

"Yes, sir. You may punish me."

"No. Your wounds are enough punishment, for now." Banshee's eye shot open once more. "I take pleasure in a moving target. Punishing you would be far too easy." Banshee couldn't believe his ears. "This is not the end, though. I have a plan. There is a storm coming, men. Soon."

Chapter 16

Shade sat in his nest of newspapers, inspecting the Earth Pouch as it hung between his paws. Something told him that it was a good idea to leave the Earth Element inside instead of holding it in his paws as well. He might drop it, or something might take it, like someone from the Dark Forces.

Or Snag.

The alley was cold and damp. Puddles and sand lay all around. Two dumpsters were on either wall, and one was against the brick wall at the end of the alley.

The alley that Shade lived in was a dead end. There was one way in, and the way in was also the way out. The other end was just a wall. The floor of the alley was asphalt. It was cracked and indented in many spots. This meant that there were plenty of drinking puddles, and also lots of piles of sand. There were also trashcans that were constantly tipping over and spilling litter all over Shade's "den". He was always putting the trash back in the cans and steadying them again.

A few weeks ago some bricks had come out of the walls, which had given Shade a perfect idea. He collected all the bricks, and put them at the bases of the two trashcans next to the dumpsters. Now they wouldn't tip over.

Now, he was enjoying lying in his tidy alley. A week had passed since he and Hurricane had fought off the raven for the second element, air.

Shade turned over and lay on his back. He looked closely at the pouch. It was a beautiful green. Not too dark, but also not too light. The embroidered "E" for "Earth" glittered a grand gold color.

Shade looked up at the sky. It was cloudy. He wondered what Hurricane was doing right now, and what he had meant by "club". Shade knew that Hurricane lived *somewhere*, and so far, the club that he had mentioned was Shade's best guess.

Shade strapped the pouch around his neck. The green ribbon had weathered a lot more than Shade had expected it to. A fight with a raven, water, getting caught on things, and more.

Shade stepped out of the alley. He began to walk down the sidewalk when he heard, "Half-mutt!"

Oh, great. Here we go again.

He turned to see Snag and his five companions running up. Just as the youngest one with a cowlick tried to splash him, Shade jumped out of the way.

"Hey!" the youngest one barked. "That's not fair! Stand still!"

"Forget it, Nox," Snag woofed to the youngest one who had attempted to splash Shade. "He's not going to stand still."

Shade decided to get back at Nox. Shade sprinted up to a puddle and splashed him.

"Hey! Snag, he got me wet!"

"Listen, Half-mutt, we're taking the alley. Either you join us, under *my* command, or be homeless. So? Which do you pick?"

"Wait, you're evicting me? You don't have a right to do that! I live here! You don't own the city!"

"In a few days time, I will." Snag leaned down to lick one of his paws. "So far, I have about a quarter of the strays in New York City under my command. They have joined us, and now we wait for the rest of the city strays to join as well."

Shade peeled back his lips in a snarl. "This isn't right! You can't just *own* every dog! Some of us want our freedom!"

"But Shade, you need to put something in perspective. Think about it: none of us will ever go hungry again! We will all rely on each other. Things will be so much easier!"

"But Snag, with such a huge pack always hunting, we will run out of prey. There'll be nothing left to eat."

"Then we will forage for garbage until the prey comes back. Simple."

"No, not simple. Dogs need fresh meat, not garbage all of the time!"

"Then we'll raid restaurant kitchens. Problem solved."

"No, that won't work, either! They'll catch one of us at some point, and maybe even call the dog catchers!"

"Look Half-mutt, if you don't think it will work, you don't have to join. Be homeless for all I care. But trust me, it would be better if you did."

Snag turned to his group. "Let Shade think about it, boys!" He turned back to Shade, "We'll be back for your decision in three days. You better be thinking." With a bark, Snag and his group galloped away.

"Nice necklace, Half-mutt!" Nox yelped as they galloped away.

"Nice cowlick, kitty-cat!" Shade barked back. Nox barked back angrily, then kept going.

You'll have my decision, Snag, don't worry. It'll be a definite no.

Chapter 17

Shade walked up the street in the opposite direction that Snag's group had gone. The Earth Pouch swayed back and forth while hanging from his neck.

"I've got to find Hurricane. It's been too long since we last got the Air Element."

Shade began to run down the street. Twilight was making its way through the afternoon, which meant that there were fewer humans. Shade began to break into a sprint when he saw a small German Shepherd mix walking into a crack in a wall. Shade looked up at the sign on the building. It read "Benny's Bar and Café". Shade smiled and walked through the crack in the wall.

When he crept into the building, he found himself in a dark storage room. Wooden crates filled the area. He squinted to see a few multi-colored lights in a corner of the room. When he got to the area, there was a long crate tipped on its side to make a bar. Above, there were some corrugated tin sheets that made an overhang. Lanterns hung from the metal sheets. The lanterns were red and yellow, giving the small space a warm, calming feeling. There were some lanterns lining the bar, and behind the bar was another crate tipped on its side with holes knocked in it for bottles to be put in. Some smaller boxes lined along the bar crate made bar chairs. A few dogs were sitting on the crates enjoying cold root beers.

Shade noticed the same Shepherd mutt standing behind the bar washing a glass sundae cup with a rag that he held in his mouth. He looked up and nodded to Shade. The dull lantern light illuminated the mutt's red bandana. He looked up and waved. "Howdy, Shade! Come on over and have a seat!"

"Thanks, Deacon," Shade answered the mutt. Shade walked over and pulled up a crate to lie on.

"So, what'll it be today, Shady? How ya feelin'? Low? Tall? Happy? Sad? Down? I got a drink for each one!"

"A little confused today, Deacon," Shade answered.

"Oh! A mixture of drinks seems appropriate, then. Alright! One Mix-'n-Match comin' right up." Deacon grabbed two bottles and a cup, shook both bottles with his teeth, and poured them into a glass. He stuck in a straw and a little umbrella, and pushed it across the bar crate towards Shade. "Here ya go."

Shade sniffed the glass. "Um, Deacon? What exactly am I drinking?"

"Root beer, shakin' up with some ice cold lemon-lime soda."

Shade looked down at his soda. He took a sip and looked at Deacon. "This actually tastes really good."

"It all depends on your mood, Shady! For instance, if you were drinking this and you felt sad, it wouldn't taste as good as it does now, when you're confused. A drink for each emotion!"

Shade smiled. "Thanks, Deac'."

"Anytime, Shady. So, you wanna pay today? Or have you even got any trade or money on you?"

"Sorry, Deacon. I don't have anything."

"How's about that knick-knack around yer neck? Looks tradable enough to me."

Shade looked at the Earth Pouch tied around his neck.

He can't have this.

"No, Deacon. I can't give you this."

"Oh, alrighty then."

Good. He didn't ask why.

Deacon's bar didn't work like other *real* bars. You paid if you felt generous. Otherwise you weren't required to. Apparently Deacon was the pet of one of the bartenders in the actual bar. Deacon had created his own bar and café for dogs in the storage room of Benny's Bar and Café. Deacon came every day, 24 hours a day, except Sundays. He tended his bar, which he called "Deacon's Doggie Diner". Not only was his bar also a café, but it was a diner as well. He had set up five square crates with four smaller crates on each side to make tables. In the middle of each table, he set a red or yellow colored lantern. He hid his diner from humans by putting a big wall of crates around it. The crack in the wall of Benny's Bar and Café was the entrance to Deacon's Doggie

Diner. It was pretty popular among the local strays. He had even hired a few waiters to tend the diner tables.

"I love this place. It's one of the *very* few places that I feel like I'm at home." Shade settled deeper into his chair with a sigh.

"Ah yes. The darkness gives it a quiet feeling, and the dull light of the lanterns make it very cozy and homey."

Shade looked at Deacon. "Um... I don't really have a reason for asking this, but... how would you feel if everything was dark? All the time?"

Deacon laughed, still looking at the sundae glass that he was scrubbing. "Dark is nice, Shady, but sometimes you can get too much of a good thing. I'd enjoy a few straight days of very dull light, but after a while, I'd enjoy the feeling of the warm sun on my back."

Shade looked down at his root beer and lemon lime Mix-'n-Match. He thought about the darkness that was overwhelming everything. Even Deacon wouldn't be able to stand the dark for too long. And he knew that there would be more than just darkness. The Dark Forces would control everything, turn everyone's hearts black and cold, and hurt anyone who disagreed.

I've got to find Hurricane.

Just as Shade turned around to leave, he saw something that made him turn right back facing the bar. He saw Snag and his group of strays cornering a young dog before sitting down. So far, they hadn't noticed Shade. He listened to what they were growling at the half-grown pup.

"Join us, you lazy mutt!" Snag ordered. "It'll be so much better than living with some little group, making their home in an alley, barely big enough for even *two* dogs to fit in!"

"I've lived with my group since I was born! The four of us are faring well enough living in our alley. We don't need to join your pack!" The pup made his voice sound strong, but Shade could see in his eyes that he was terrified.

"You are *required* to join our pack! Every stray in New York is!"

67

Shade could tell that the pup had no idea what he was supposed to say. He made a stuttering sound in his throat before speaking again. "Ah… I… ah…uh…"

"Talk!"

"I don't know!" He finally barked. "I don't make the decisions in my group! I'm the youngest of the four!"

"Then take us to your group later. We need some drinks first." Snag led the way to a crate table. One of the dogs in his group grabbed the pup by his scruff and dragged him to the table. Since there were only four crate seats, Snag said that he and the other three dogs would sit while the one dragging the pup would keep an eye on him.

"I never understood Snag," Deacon commented.

Shade looked at Deacon. "Has he asked you to join his pack yet?"

"Nope, 'cause he knows I belong to a human. Everybody does. But if I was a stray, he'd probably be paying every time he came, *just* to get me to join this thang."

"Good for you. He already asked me. Well, I wouldn't call it 'asking', more like 'demanding'. He's given me three days for my answer."

"Yikes. Well, best of luck to ya. Another drink?"

Shade turned to see Snag's group. They wouldn't be leaving anytime soon.

I'll get to Hurricane once these guys are out of my way. I can't risk being cornered for my decision like that pup.

Shade sighed. "Sure, Deacon. Make this drink for someone who's frustrated."

Chapter 18

After waiting almost two hours, drinking five and a half more drinks, and having a long conversation all the while with the other strays and Deacon, Shade was finally able to leave. Snag had told his five dogs that the pup was going to take them to his group, and he ordered the pup to do so. With that, they all left. Shade grabbed a few shiny rocks he found outside Deacon's Doggie Diner on the sidewalk and gave them to Deacon as a way to say "thanks for all the drinks". So, apparently, Shade paid after all.

Now he was walking down the sidewalk toward the abandoned house. He waited for Hurricane to pop up somewhere, maybe with Lexie or another cat, but he never did. Shade got all the way to the weed filled yard of the abandoned house, and never even caught a glimpse of the black tom.

Will Everest appear if Hurricane isn't with me?

Shade took one last look both ways down the sidewalk, and padded inside.

"Hurricane?" he barked quietly. He wondered if Hurricane was already here. "Hurricane, quit it. I'm not here to play games. Come out!"

Silence.

Shade felt dizzy.

"Everest? Are you here? Is *anyone* here?" Shade suddenly felt scared. The abandoned house was dark and spooky, and without someone else there, he felt extremely vulnerable. He had to get out of there.

Shade whipped around. He ran for the door, but for some reason it felt like the faster he ran towards it, the farther away it went. Suddenly, fire exploded in front of Shade's eyes. He was trapped in a ring of fire. The living room of the abandoned house disappeared, and was replaced by nothing but black. The only light was the fire, casting an orange, red, and yellow glow.

"Help! Somebody help me!" Shade's barking echoed around him and faded into the black nothingness. His screams were heard by no one, and were accompanied by the crackles and hisses of the fire.

"Once I'm finished, no one will be able to help you," a deep voice bellowed.

Shade turned in all directions. There was nobody to be seen.

"You think that you will find the elements before me? Ha! As if. I would never let someone destroy my chance of ruling this pitiful planet. I will destroy you, and then every other in turn! You can't defeat me!"

Shade kept turning. The voice came from every direction, but nobody was there. "No! We *will* find the four elements first! You're one of the Dark Forces, aren't you?"

The voice boomed once more. "One of the Dark Forces? I'm not *just* one of the Dark Forces, I am the lord of them all!"

A huge red and black dragon appeared in front of Shade's vision. A black staff with a red glowing jewel at the tip was clasped in his cruel claws. "I am the Dark Lord, the Lord of Eternal Darkness!" The dragon flew up to Shade's firetrap, and looked Shade in the eye. "Why, Shade?" He asked with a booming voice. "Why don't you join the dark side? All it takes is a bit of anger and sadness, a few bad memories... you can be one of us, wolf."

Shade snarled at the Dark Lord.

"You are filled with anger and sadness, Shade. *Filled* with horrible memories of betrayal and hurt. Use that anger to your advantage. You can turn it into a weapon. That weapon can be used to rule everything and everyone!"

Shade heard a voice behind him, yelling.

Everest?

"Shade! No! Don't listen to him! He's using you!" Shade turned to see Everest, standing in the middle of the black nothingness.

"Everest!" Shade barked.

"Hmmm... is that your friend?" The Dark Lord blew a long line of fire towards Everest.

"No! You'll kill him!" Shade cried out.

"Don't worry, he'll be fine. He's just in a fire ring, like you."

"Everest! Are you alright?"

"I'm fine!" Everest replied.

Shade felt like screaming, but that might just make the Dark Lord angry. Shade had to think of something.

"Shade, you have so much hatred, sadness, anger. Why don't you just let it out? So many horrible memories... are all of those going to go to waste?"

Shade tried to block out the Dark Lord. He knew he shouldn't listen, but it was almost impossible. The Dark Lord was voicing Shade's everyday thoughts, the things that he always tried so hard to keep in. It was almost painful for the Dark Lord to remind him of it all.

"Let us take a walk down Memory Lane, shall we?" the Dark Lord growled.

With the bang of his staff on the black ground, the Dark Lord sent the two of them to a rundown cabin at the edge of a forest. Farther behind them were the skyscrapers of New York.

"Where are we?" Shade asked the Dark Lord.

"Trust me, in a few moments, the memory of the events that happened here will come flooding back to you."

Suddenly, a huge, male, gray wolf emerged from the undergrowth in the forest.

"Who's he?" Shade asked.

"Someone very close to you," the Dark Lord answered.

Then a smaller pointy-eared dog came into sight, walking from the direction of the city. As she came closer, Shade could see that she was carrying something gray and black.

"Is that... Who *is* that?"

"You'll see in a few moments," the Dark Lord replied.

As she came closer, realization slammed into Shade.

"Mother!" he yelped. He tried running towards her, but she took no notice. She only kept walking towards the gray wolf.

"Don't try, Shade. Neither of them can see you. This is simply a flashback." The Dark Lord twirled his staff.

Shade and the Dark Lord walked closer to the two canines. Shade looked at the gray and black bundle to realize that it was a puppy.

"Is that…" Shade turned his head to the Dark Lord. "Is that me?"

The Dark Lord grinned an evil grin and nodded his head.

The small black and brown dog that was Shade's mother spoke. "This is your son, Rebel." She set him down on the ground in front of her paws.

The gray wolf looked down at the puppy-Shade. "My son?" The wolf walked forward and touched noses with the pup.

Shade felt it.

"He'll be great for raising in a pack! He looks cut out to be a great runner. Strong and smart-looking, too."

"Rebel, I'm keeping him."

Rebel looked up. "What?"

"I don't trust you anymore. After the last battle you had with your rival pack, I realized that safety wasn't exactly a priority for you. And I also don't trust you, personally."

"What? Why?"

"Because of your personality. You're reckless, and you take too many risks. I'm not letting you raise him. I will, and he'll learn to be a dog, not a wolf."

"But Eclipse! He's both! And don't you love me?"

"Of course I do. But it will never be that easy."

"Yes it can! You can join my pack!"

"They won't just accept me, Rebel. And they won't easily accept our son, either. Besides, I prefer the city."

"But… but… He's my son too!"

"I know, Rebel. I know. But I don't want him in the forest. He's in too much danger there."

Rebel's eyes lit with a mixture of anger and sadness. "How can you keep me from my own son?"

"I'm sorry, Rebel. But I'm not letting him live in the wolf pack."

"Fine then! Keep him locked away in the city! But you wait. One day, he'll be drawn to the forest himself! He'll figure out who he is and come find his father!" Rebel began to turn back to the forest when suddenly he stopped. "Eclipse, at least tell me what his name is."

Shade stood beside the Dark Lord, listening to the whole conversation. He couldn't believe what he was hearing. He looked down at his puppy-self, who was completely unaware of what was happening. He just kept looking at Rebel.

Eclipse, Shade's mother, looked down at the puppy-Shade. "Sh… Shade… yes. His name is Shade."

"Shade," Rebel, Shade's father, echoed. "Shade." He touched noses with the puppy-Shade once more.

Shade felt it again.

Rebel looked up at Eclipse for the last time. With the flick of his tail and a last love-filled glance at the two of them, he spun around and disappeared into the forest.

Eclipse stared after him for a moment, then picked up the puppy-Shade and began to leave. To Shade's surprise, his puppy face seemed to fall as he watched his father leave. His puppy-self even let out a small wail, as though he knew that was his father.

Had he known?

"Sad enough for you Shade?" the Dark Lord asked. "The memory of being torn from your own father?"

"It was… interesting. Sort of… depressing."

"Excellent! Exactly what I wanted to hear. Now, I have two more treats for you." The Dark Lord banged his staff on the ground. Suddenly, they were swept away to the busy streets of New York.

A taxi was parked on the street as a couple got in. The moment it pulled away, two faces popped out from around a corner store.

Shade suddenly remembered this place. "No! Take me away from here! I can't stand to go through this all over again!"

The Dark Lord laughed to himself.

The two faces revealed themselves to be Shade's mother, Eclipse, and a half-grown Shade.

"Follow me, Shade. There's good food just up the street."

"Okay, Mama," Shade's young-self answered.

"No!" Shade ran up to his younger self. "Don't say that! You'll only coax her on!" He ran to Eclipse. "Don't! It's not safe there! Please don't go!"

The Dark Lord laughed. "She can't hear you, Shade. Like I said. This is simply a flashback, an *illusion* if you will. No point in trying."

"Eclipse! Please! Don't!" Shade leaped in front of her, trying to block the way, but she walked *right through him.*

"What the…"

"I told you Shade, no use in trying," the Dark Lord gloated.

Shade and the Dark Lord followed the two down the sidewalk. "Please stop," Shade whispered.

"There!" Shade's mother finally said. "In that trashcan. I found a whole chicken! I wanted to surprise you."

"Wow! Really?" the young Shade exclaimed.

"Of course! You go first, Shade."

The young Shade bounced over to the can and tipped it over. A huge baked chicken spilled out. "Yes! A feast!"

"Exactly." Eclipse walked over to grab the chicken. "Let's take this back to our alley-den."

"Okay!"

The two began walking once again. Shade knew that the devastating event was going to happen now. "I can't look." Shade looked away.

"No, Shade. You are required to look," the Dark Lord growled, grinning.

Shade opened his eyes just as the truck came around the corner. Eclipse took a moment to notice it, but when she did, she spun around and shoved the puppy-Shade backwards, dropping the chicken. "Run! Now!"

The puppy-Shade stood there, bewildered. "Why?"

"Dogcatcher! Run!"

"Wait, dogcatcher? No!"

Puppy-Shade and Eclipse began to make their way down the street. The dogcatcher leaped out of his truck and ran after the two dogs.

Eclipse barked to Puppy-Shade. "Run. We can't both get away. But maybe I can create a distraction while you make a run for it."

"What? No! I can't just leave you here!"

"I'll catch up with you later. Just run back to the den!"

"You promise that I'll see you again? You'll come back to the den before tonight?"

Eclipse looked at Puppy-Shade for a moment as they ran down the sidewalk. Shade could tell by her eyes that she knew that wouldn't be happening. "Run. Now."

"Do you promise you'll come back before night comes?" Puppy-Shade insisted.

"Run, Shade! Now!"

Puppy-Shade let out a wail, and ran ahead as his mother spun around and ran at the pursuing dogcatcher. Shade and the Dark Lord stopped running, and stood watching as Eclipse sprang at the dogcatcher. But with a quick slap across her face, Eclipse was on the ground. The dogcatcher took his special leash and strapped it around Eclipse's neck. She snarled and barked, only to be dragged away, and thrown into the mouth of the truck.

Shade hung his head. The Dark Lord laughed. "Well that was certainly exciting! What say we give her a nice send-off?" The Dark Lord waved a claw after her. Shade began following the truck.

"Where are you going, wolf?" the Dark Lord asked.

Shade didn't answer.

"Well then? What say we leave here?"

Shade growled. "Not yet."

"Yes, now," the Dark Lord demanded. "I am anticipating seeing your face when Eclipse doesn't return tonight."

Shade's face fell. "Do we have to?"

The Dark Lord chuckled. "I certainly want to. Let's flash forward a few hours to when the sun and moon share the sky, eh?" With the bang of his staff, the two of them were flash forwarded to twilight. Shade looked down to see his younger-self curled in a pile of brown leaves. This was the same alley that he lived in now.

"Would you like to read your young self's thoughts, Shade?" the Dark Lord snickered.

Shade didn't need to. He remembered what had gone through his head that night.

"I want to. I *really* want to." The Dark Lord put his staff to the young Shade's head, and with a slow twirl of it, the two of them could hear exactly what Puppy-Shade was thinking.

She'll be back. She always comes back. She fought off a group of dogs once and came back. She'll come back this time too.

The group of dogs that Puppy-Shade was referring to in his thoughts was Snag's group. Though at the time, the leader of the group

76

was Snag's uncle who had taken care of Snag when he was a puppy. Shade never knew what had happened to Snag's parents, but Snag's uncle, Slash, had raised him. When Slash retired, Snag was recruited to leader of the group, and soon, he would be leader of everything in New York. Slash must be proud.

Shade shook his head at himself. "She's not coming back, idiot."

"Like I've said many times before Shade, they can't hear you," the Dark Lord reminded Shade.

Shade sat down on the asphalt ground. He heard a rumbling noise and looked up, immediately knowing what it was. Puppy-Shade looked up as well.

The dogcatcher truck rumbled by, Eclipse's depressed face looking out. Puppy-Shade let out a horrified yelp and scrambled after the truck. Eclipse flattened back her ears. "No, Shade! Stay here! It's not safe for you to follow. I'm sorry." With that, the truck gained speed and careened around the corner.

"No!" Puppy-Shade cried at the top of his lungs. He crumpled onto the sidewalk, barely holding back tears.

"Why didn't you just break down and start crying?" the Dark Lord sneered.

"I didn't think it was right. I knew that I had to get over it and just go on."

"How brave. Well, I believe that we only have one more quick stop." The Dark Lord banged his staff for the last time. They were swept to a few weeks ago, right before he tumbled into Hurricane. He was being taunted by Snag's group, mainly being splashed and called Half-mutt by the youngest one, Nox.

"Remember this?" the Dark Lord asked.

"Yes. Snag's group is like a broken record. Same taunts, same words, same actions. I can't believe that I can actually pick this one out specifically from all of the times that they bullied me."

"Really? Excellent. Let us watch this little play, shall we?" The Dark Lord sat down, folding his wings.

Shade and the Dark Lord watched the whole commotion before Shade ran away just as Snag's group was leaping on him.

"Well that was fun! Let's go back to the house, now. This is getting tiring."

With a flash of bright light, the street was gone, replaced by a black space and a firewall.

Chapter 19

Shade stood, blinking, in the ring of fire. The Dark Lord bowed over him, casting a long dark shadow.

"Well, wasn't that fun? It's good to recall old memories now and then," the Dark Lord mocked. He leaned closer to Shade. "Even if those memories chill your heart."

Shade snarled at the Dark Lord. "Why did you even show me any of that?"

"Shade, Shade, Shade. Haven't you learned anything in this short time?" The Dark Lord grinned menacingly. "What about you, Everest?" The Dark Lord motioned to the dog with an eye-patch in the fire ring next to Shade's. "Why do you think I showed him these awful visions?"

Everest stared angrily into the eyes of the Dark Lord. The fur on his back stood straight up, and he scraped his claws along the black floor. "Unlock us from these traps, and I will answer your question."

"Sorry, Everest. That's not an option."

Everest barked at the Lord of Eternal Darkness. "Unleash us!"

The Dark Lord's red eyes blazed with a sudden spark of anger. With a mighty flap of his red wings, he lifted himself up into the darkness of the completely black room. "You will not order me to do the things that you wish! Here, now, *I* am the one in charge! Now, answer!"

Shade spoke before Everest could utter a word. "Where are we? We're not in the abandoned house anymore. Everything is jet-black. The walls, the floor, and the ceiling. The only objects here are the two fire rings and us. Tell us where we are, and we'll answer your questions."

The Dark Lord stopped flapping and hit the floor with a loud bang. The ground shook. "Fine then." He threw his staff down next to him. "You are still in the abandoned house. Though I have made the walls and furniture disappear, and replaced it with this dark room. Are you happy now? Maybe one of you will answer my question. Everest, why did I show Shade his past?"

Everest snorted. "You were trying to make him angry."

"Exactly. And why would I do that? Do you know?"

"So that when he was visibly able to recall all the anger that built up inside him throughout his life, he could use it as a weapon."

"A weapon to do what?" the Dark Lord pressed on.

"To get his way and become more powerful."

"Wonderful explanation, Everest. Would you like to see one of *your* bad memories?" The Dark Lord picked up his staff.

"Everest, no!" Shade cried. The Dark Lord had been correct when he said that the memories would change him. Shade felt almost furious. The same couldn't happen to Everest.

Everest backed up toward the other end of his fire ring. He shook his head. "No. No, I won't let you."

"Sorry, that's my call to make, and you're seeing it." The Dark Lord banged his staff on the ground, and the two of them suddenly stood still. *Completely* still.

Everest's good blue eye began glowing, casting a blue light on the orange flames of the fire ring. A dim blue light could be seen through his eye patch.

So, when I went to my flashback, I didn't actually go anywhere? I just stood here, and it was all in my mind? That's when Shade realized something. The Dark Lord hadn't really taken him anywhere. He was just able to get inside his mind and strike fear through him. *It was all in my head! That's how the Dark Lord and the rest of the Dark Forces control you. They just get in your head and make you scared enough to listen to them.*

"It was a mind trick..." Shade whispered to himself.

The Dark Lord suddenly stopped staring and looked at Shade. "Come along, Shade. This flashback will be interesting, I assure you." The Dark Lord waved his staff at Shade's head. A red haze began clouding his vision, and suddenly there was nothing but a rich crimson.

Chapter 20

All around Shade, there were fighting dogs. All of the dogs were covered in blood, giving the impression that this battle had been going on for days. Everest was standing stock-still, staring at the battle as though it was a magnet for his eye. He crouched down, ears flattened, his good eye wide and blazing with fear.

"Where are we?" Shade asked.

"A little memory from Everest's past," the Dark Lord sneered.

Everest refused to move.

"Everest? Where are we?"

Everest turned his head to Shade. "We're in the midst of one of the biggest battles in Sighter Dog history."

The three of them stood on a very low ridge, slightly overlooking the battle. "What's it about?"

Everest trembled. "The Rocky Mountains had been taken over by a huge force of rebelling Sighter Dogs. They saw no point in looking after the Earth without anyone knowing that they were even there. They wanted to control the Earth instead of protecting it. They thought that the only way to get the rest of the Sighter Dogs across the planet to join them was to take the Rocky Mountains for themselves, the most important mountains to every Sighter Dog in the world. The Sighter Dogs that hadn't been taken over by ambition knew that the only way to get the mountains back was to fight them." Everest looked back at the battle. "I was a student at the time. This is how I lost my left eye."

Shade cringed.

"Hmm..." the Dark Lord mumbled. "I believe that this will take a while. What say we skip right to the point?" The Dark Lord whirled his staff at the scene, and suddenly the area looked darker. The whole sky was overcast, even drizzling a bit. So, none of them could tell what time of day it was.

"What time is it now?" Shade asked.

"I flashed us a few hours forward. It's twilight now." The Dark Lord stood up and started walking toward the battle. "Come along. There is something you both must see."

They began walking right into the midst of the battle. Dogs were actually leaping *through* Shade. He winced each time he witnessed a dog leaping onto another one, or clamping down hard on each other with their merciless fangs. Shade stepped through puddles of water mixed with blood. The clouds suddenly opened up, and a downpour of rain came falling down on the dogs. Shade shivered.

"I'm cold," he commented.

The Dark Lord let out a mocking laugh. "You've fought off a raven before, and you're complaining about a little late autumn chill? Let's put things in perspective, shall we?"

*   *   *   *   *   *   *   *

A long hour of walking passed. The whole way, the rain would only come down harder and harder. When the three finally came to a stop, before them stood a bare tree. It's limbs hung sadly, and only a few pathetic brown leaves clung to its branches. There seemed to be a fox or a badger den in-between the mangled roots. A small dog, probably a German Shepherd mix, was running in and out of the hole. She went in with a bundle of leaves and moss, and then came out with nothing. She then grabbed more leaves and moss from the base of the tree, and scuttled back inside, then the whole ordeal was done again.

"Who's that?" Shade asked.

"That," Everest began, "was my mentor."

Shade nodded. A student couldn't be a student without someone to teach them all they need to know.

The Dark Lord nudged both of them forward. "Take a look inside," he insisted. Everest eyes suddenly seemed to light up with realization.

"I remember this tree!" he exclaimed.

"Good. Now look inside."

82

Everest scuffled forward unwillingly. Shade followed, not knowing what to expect.

When Shade looked inside, what he saw made him yelp and jump backwards. Everest stayed put, and watched.

The Dark Lord looked down at the half-wolf-half-dog. "Look," he ordered.

Reluctantly, Shade took a peek back inside. He cringed at the sight. There lay a very young Everest. He was lying on his side, breathing deeply and coughing blood. His mentor had created a nest for him. Now she was sitting next to him. Her worried gaze fell on the young Everest. But it wasn't the fact that Everest was coughing blood. What made Shade cringe was that the whole left side of Everest's face was bleeding out. His right eye was wild with fear, and the young Everest wouldn't stop asking about why he could only see out of one eye. His mentor seemed unsure of what to say.

"You've lost an eye, young one," she said, trembling.

Everest winced in shock. He kicked out with his back legs. "No! No! How could this happen? I can't have lost an eye! I'll never see the same way again!" The young Everest let out a sudden gasp of pain. "I want to kill that dog! Let me fight him! I can't let him get away with this!"

His mentor shook her head. "No, Everest. You'll lose more blood."

"Please, Klondike! Let me destroy that dog!"

Everest's mentor shook her head more sternly. "No. I won't let you. You're already too weak, and you've lost enough blood as it is. You need rest. We're safe in here.

"No we're not! The battle is only a few yards away!"

Then Klondike did something amazing. She *whacked* poor Everest on the head.

"What the... why'd she do that?" Shade asked.

Everest shook his head. "In a battle, words can't always control the mind. Sometimes demands have to be expressed through a whack on the head."

Shade looked at the student now. He had stopped writhing and talking. "Oh."

"Well," the Dark Lord began, "I think that's all we needed to see. Let's get back."

With a twirl of his staff, the Dark Lord submerged them back into darkness, held against their will within rings of crackling flames.

Chapter 21

Shade looked over to where Everest was held prisoner in his own firetrap.

"Well, it's been fun, but I'm afraid we must part. Good day to you both." The Dark Lord began raising his staff above his massive head. "Don't become too comfortable, though," he grinned menacingly, "for you both will be seeing me soon." He brought his staff down so hard that the ground beneath their feet rumbled. A blinding red light appeared from the ruby jewel at the tip of his staff. Soon the black room was completely covered by the blinding red glow. Then suddenly, a blast of wind knocked both dogs off of their feet. They hit the ground with a great thump.

When Shade opened his eyes, still wincing from the impact with the ground, he found that he was lying on the oval rug. "Everest?" he croaked out.

"Over here, Shade."

Shade turned his head to see Everest lying on the wood floor a few yards away from him. "Everest? Are you okay?"

"I'm fine, Shade. We're back in the abandoned house." Everest lifted himself up. "We're safe, for now."

For now? Shade thought.

"Where could Hurricane be? He missed a lot." Shade walked to the door. Hurricane was nowhere to be seen.

Everest shrugged. "I don't know. He could be anywhere. He's a cat, what do you expect?"

Suddenly, Shade had an awful thought. "What if the Dark Forces have taken him prisoner?"

Everest's eyes seemed to light up with anxiety for a moment, but soon the look disappeared. "I doubt it. At the moment, the Dark Lord and his army of Dark Forces are trying to get us to come over to their side. Imprisoning someone of our own would only make becoming one of them less appealing."

Shade flattened his ears. "I don't know…" He still felt uneasy.

"Why don't you go look for him? He has to live somewhere."

Shade's eyes brightened. "Okay, come on." Shade motioned towards the door.

Everest shook his head. "Shade, I'm a Sighter Dog. I can't just walk out into the open."

Shade's head hung a tad lower. "Come on, Everest. No one even knows that Sighter Dogs exist, much less what they even are."

Everest turned his head to show Shade his left side. "What about my eye-patch? It will give something away."

"So what if you have an eye-patch?" Shade huffed. "They'll just come to the conclusion that you lost an eye. Which you did. Or that you're really obsessed with pirates."

"What about all of my scars? They're all over me."

"Everest, *all* the dogs around here have scars. Even me."

"Not as many as I have."

"Actually, there are a few dogs around here with close to that many scars. Also, in this part of the city, you're looked up to if you have a lot of battle scars. It means that you have more fighting experience." Shade looked at the single three long claw marks on his right flank. They were almost invisible now, barely completely covered by fur. They had stopped hurting a long time ago. "As you can see, I'm not really looked up to, or seen as any type of authority. Less scars, less respect. More scars, more authority."

"So the dogs here carry their scars as trophies?"

"Pretty much."

Everest sighed. "Fine. I'll help you look for Hurricane. But don't expect this type of outcome all the time."

The two of them walked out into the overcast city. "Why is it always cloudy here?" Everest asked.

86

"Smog. It's getting pretty polluted in these parts. But I suppose it's better than the blinding sun all day, otherwise we'd all be sweating like pigs."

"Um, excuse my logic, but pigs don't sweat. That's why they roll in the mud."

Shade rolled his eyes. "No need for a scientific explanation, genius."

Everest laughed. "I know, I know. Let's just keep walking."

Shade turned at the sidewalk. "Hurricane said something about a club. Like, he lives there, I guess."

"Hmm..." Everest mumbled. "Well, I expect that there should be an entrance somewhere, and it can't be far if you two always meet to go to the abandoned house."

"An entrance." That gave Shade an idea. "We should go to Deacon's Doggie Diner. Deacon knows everyone."

"But," Everest began, "if it's called Deacon's *Doggie* Diner, doesn't that mean that only dogs go there?"

Shade thought for a moment. "Let's give it a try, anyway. Deacon would let anyone into his diner. He's a social dog."

Everest shrugged. "Whatever you say."

Shade and Everest padded down the sidewalk, Shade explaining a bit more about the diner the whole way. The big *Benny's Bar and Café* sign finally came into sight. "There it is, Everest."

"Wow. This Deacon's got quite a set up for dogs that don't even always pay."

"Everest, that's where the *actual* diner is. I told you, Deacon made his diner and café in the storage room of the actual bar."

Everest laughed at himself. "Oh, right."

Shade squeezed through the crack in the wall that led to Deacon's bar. "Deacon? You open?"

Shade heard the familiar country accent from around some crates. A dull red glow illuminated the corner where the diner/bar/café was. "Twenty-four hours a day, six days a week, Ol' Shady!"

Shade smiled and walked through the entrance, Everest coming in behind him.

Shade swerved through a few old crates and finally emerged into the enclosed space. Wooden crates worked as walls so that humans wouldn't see the set up. "What'll it be, Shady? Oh! You brought a friend. Well, he's welcome to have a drink, too!"

Everest glanced sideways at Shade. "I suppose you were right about the social part, but how is he with cats?"

"I'm great with cats. Why ya wonderin'? I'm still four years old so don't bother whisperin'. I can hear ya right fine."

Shade cleared his throat. The Earth Pouch around his neck swayed. "Have you heard of Hurricane? He's a black cat. Sort of grumpy."

Deacon's eyes brightened. "By Jove! I swear I've heard that name somewhere once er twice."

"Really?" Shade and Everest asked in unison.

"Well a' course. That little fur ball comes here every now and then."

"Great! Do you know where he lives?" Shade asked impatiently.

"Now hang on just a minute. You two pull up a crate and tell me why you need to find the little fuzzy guy."

Shade rolled his eyes and lay down on a crate. Everest did the same. Deacon sat down on his haunches on the other side of the long rectangular crate that created the bar. "Alright. Now tell me why ya'll need to find Hurricane."

Shade looked at Everest. They couldn't tell Deacon about the everlasting darkness. He would spread the word to his customers. Shade knew that he would, because Deacon had a bad tendency to run his mouth. Then once the news was spread to everyone, they would all panic. They couldn't let that happen. Not to mention, Everest's identity would be given away.

"Um," Everest stuttered.

"We have to return something to him," Shade quickly answered.

"Really? What do you have to give to him? I don't want you makin' up some excuse just to chase a cat around the city fer yer enjoyment."

"Chasing him around?" Deacon totally had the wrong idea. "He's our friend! Why would we want to chase him around?"

"Yer a dog, and he's a cat."

Deacon had a point. "We're not just trying to figure out where he lives so that we can chase him for fun. We have to give something back to him."

"What do ya have to give back to him? Show me."

Shade glanced at Everest, who began frantically nosing under the bar.

"Hey, Deac'? Could you get my friend," Shade looked at Everest snuffling under the bar, "Butch, here a water? Me too."

Deacon creased his brow. "Shade? Show me."

"I will! Butch is looking for it."

Deacon gave Shade a suspicious look, then turned to pour them two waters.

Shade swung his head downwards. "What are you doing?" he whispered exasperatedly.

"Looking for something to show to Deacon! Dogs have dropped tons of stuff under here."

Shade lifted his head. Deacon had finished filling one glass, and was sticking a lime in it.

"Hurry! He's almost done pouring our waters!"

Deacon set the first glass down. "This is yers, Shady." He turned to pour Everest's.

"Hurry up, Everest! Pick something!"

Everest kept looking under the bar. "What would a cat own?"

Shade growled and grabbed a rubber ball in his teeth. He set it down on the table just as Deacon was giving Everest his water.

"This one's yers, Butch." Deacon looked down at the rubber ball. "This is what yer returning?

"Yes!" They both exclaimed.

"Okay, okay! He lives in a club down the street. It's a crack in the wall at Mario's Italian Cuisine. The crack's the entrance to a storage room, where the club is. The club only allows cats to join it. Some cat named Fletch runs the club. That's why the club is called the Fletch Cat Club."

"Thanks, Deacon. That really helps." The two took a last sip of their waters and began to leave.

"Wait!" Deacon exclaimed.

Shade and Everest turned around, blinking.

"There's a password. You can't get in without knowing it. There're always two guards that demand it."

Shade moaned. A password? Really? "Do you know what it is?"

"No idea," Deacon said, scrubbing a glass with a rag that he held in his teeth. "But can't ya just give the silly ball to the two guards at the entrance and tell 'em to give it to him?"

Shade shared a glance with Everest. "Good idea, Deacon. We'll do that."

"Glad I could be of assistance, fellas."

Shade and Everest left Deacon's diner. "Well, now what?" Everest asked Shade.

"I guess we go down the street and wait till we come across Mario's Italian Cuisine."

Shade and Everest padded down the cool sidewalk. "Brrrr. November is nearly over. We should be expecting the big snowstorms of New York pretty soon. I can't wait till Thanksgiving. All that food. Yum."

"The strays get together and celebrate Thanksgiving?" Everest asked.

"Yep. Well, the ones that like each other, anyway."

"Who do you usually spend Thanksgiving with?" Everest asked, turning his head toward Shade as he walked.

"Usually the dogs in the alley on the other side of the right building that creates my alley. But sometimes I just catch as much as I can and celebrate Thanksgiving alone, in my alley. I'm not exactly popular among the other dogs."

"But you're half wolf. Wouldn't they be looking up to you? Or at least a bit afraid to challenge you?"

"You'd think so, but not really. I'm more of an outcast than anything else. All other dogs on the edge of the city are all mutts, not wolves. I don't know why they don't accept me, though. I act quite a bit more like a dog. Thing is, no matter how much I act like a dog, I'll always look more like a wolf."

Everest made a muffled, "hmm," in his throat, and kept walking.

Finally, a big *Mario's Italian Cuisine* sign came into sight. The two of them stopped.

"Well, there it is," Shade woofed. "Any ideas how to get in?"

"We could go through the front door."

"We'll draw attention from humans. What about the back?"

Everest grinned. "Good idea. Let's go."

Chapter 22

Shade tiptoed through an alley to the left of the building. The other side of the restaurant was just a street corner. Shade and Everest would have to take the alley to remain unseen.

Everest nudged Shade with his nose. "Are you sure this is a good idea? I feel like we should just go around to the right of the building."

"The right side is the curb. We've exposed ourselves enough already by nonchalantly walking down the sidewalk to get here. Let's take the alley and not risk being caught by some stupid dogcatcher or a person." Shade sniffed the air. "I smell a cat or two, but that's normal, knowing that dozens of them are living in the restaurant."

Everest looked behind himself, then forward again. "Still, I feel like someone is watching us."

Shade huffed. "Everest, if someone is watching us, it's probably some idiot cat."

Suddenly, two cats dropped down in front of them *from the sky*. "Well, these two *idiot cats* are wondering what you're doing in our alley."

Shade jumped backwards with a yelp when the cats fell in front of them. One was a large light brown tabby, and the other was a black and white tuxedo cat that was only a tad smaller.

Shade and Everest looked up. Six other cats were perched on the roof of the pottery shop to their left. Their tails whipped back and forth as they crouched on the roof, ready to leap down if they had to. Devilish grins sprawled across their faces.

Shade looked back to the two cats as Everest kept an eye on the ones on the pottery shop roof. "What are your names?" Shade growled.

"Whoa now, lil' doggie," the black and white one hissed. "You're in our territory, now. We have the right to ask *you* the questions." The cat licked his lips before speaking again. He stood with his fur bristling. "What are *your* names?"

Shade snarled a threat. The cat still stood there, calmly looking at him. The light brown tabby suddenly walked up. He was huge. "You better answer that, mutt. We've got more pressing matters to deal with than tussling with you. But we will if you don't cooperate."

Shade looked at Everest, who had torn his eye from the cats on the roof. Everest shrugged. Shade turned to the cats once more. "My name is Shade. This is my companion," Shade cleared his throat, "Butch. We're looking for a cat named Hurricane. We-"

"Hurricane? What do you want with him?"

"Tell us your names, and we'll answer that."

The tabby spat at Shade, and then turned to the tuxedo cat. The cats on the roof seemed to crouch lower. The tabby whispered something to the tuxedo cat, and the tuxedo cat whispered something back. The tabby nodded, and they both turned back to Shade and Everest. "My name is Link," the tabby said. He turned to the tuxedo cat. "And this is Jax."

Shade nodded. "Good. Now, what say we start this over, eh? Ahem. My name is Shade. This is my friend Butch. What are your names?"

Link creased his brow even more. He hissed, and Shade raised an eyebrow. Link sighed. "My name is Link."

Jax pushed past him eagerly. "And I'm Jax!"

Shade could tell now that Jax was quite a bit younger than Link. "Very good. And your friends up on the roof? What are their names?"

Link growled.

"Well?" Shade pressed on.

"The silver tabby she-cat is named Silver, the white she-cat with one blue eye and one white eye and black tips on her paws ears and tail is Dream Catcher, the gray tom is Stormy, the black she-cat with white speckles is Silent Night, because the song Silent Night is a winter song and in winter it snows and at night it's black and…" Jax saw Shade constantly getting more and more bored. "Oh, sorry. Anyways, the yellow one with a white blaze down his face is Beach, and the orange and black tom is Torch!" Jax let out a breath. "Wow!"

He turned to see Link staring at him angrily with his tail whipping back and forth. "Did I say you could tell them?"

93

"Well, you never said I couldn't!" Jax countered.

Shade glanced at Everest. The scarred mutt pretended to snore. Shade smiled and held back a laugh.

"Well," Link said, turning back to the two canines, "now that we've *so generously* given you our names, will you tell us why you need Hurricane?"

"Uh," Shade looked down the alley to see a crack in the wall. A dim light was coming out of it. *That must be the entrance.* He looked back down at Link and Jax. "We need to tell him something."

"Then you can tell us. We'll pass the message on to him."

"We need to tell him ourselves."

"Why? So you can get the chance to kidnap him for your dinner? No way. We're not letting two *dogs* into our club."

"What if it was a life or death situation?" Shade growled. Link's eyes widened.

"Is it?"

Suddenly, two cats leaped down from the roof. It was Torch and Dream Catcher. "Life or death situation?" Her blue and white eyes seemed to light up with anger. "If it is, why do you want Hurricane to be involved?"

Torch pulled her back. His orange pelt stood out in the darkness of the alley. But his black patches disappeared in it. "Stand back. They're dogs. They could seriously hurt you."

"Yes, we could," Shade growled. "So let us through!"

"Look. Truth is, Hurricane isn't even here." Link licked a paw, and then passed it over his whiskers.

"What? Where is he?"

"No idea. He's been gone for three days now."

"Did you see him go somewhere?" Shade asked, fear gripping him.

"He said that he was going hunting one night. Jax and I waited forever, but he never came back. His friend, Lexie, is worried sick about him. For the last three days she's constantly been coming out here to ask if we've seen him," Link informed them.

"He probably got caught by a human," Jax said with a worried expression. Hurricane was, after all, one of his companions.

Shade looked at Everest. The two of them were trembling. A thought suddenly came to Shade. "Oh no."

Destiny

Water:
Volume IV

Chapter 23

Three Days Earlier

Hurricane curled into his bed. The sack felt hard and uncomfortable as he tried to settle in. His belly rumbled, reminding him that he still had not eaten anything for dinner.

With a groan of protest, Hurricane heaved himself out of his bed. The towel that he used as a blanket went sprawling out onto the cold wooden floor. He padded toward the cardboard box that was used as a place to stock food.

"Sorry, excuse me," Hurricane said over and over as he stepped over rows of cats settling down in their beds for the night. The restaurant had closed, so all the lights were off. This was always the signal that it was time to sleep. Luckily, since some cats liked to hang out and chat at night, Fletch and his guards had fished out three lanterns from the shelves that were all around the square-shaped space.

Hurricane looked up at the shelf near the wheelbarrow. At the very top, Fletch had made his "office". He slept there, and spent most of the day there. Sometimes he would climb down the shelf and weave through the crowds of club cats, who would each formally greet their leader. He would nod to each of them in turn, and keep walking. Hurricane believed that he did this to get attention, but Fletch claimed that he was doing it to check on his club companions, and to get a bite to eat. Hurricane knew that Fletch had guards to keep an eye on the club's status, and Fletch had servants to bring him food. Though, Hurricane also knew that Fletch wouldn't be able to stay up on a dusty old shelf alone forever, so he would have to come down every once in a while to mingle with friends.

Hurricane finally got over to the stockpile to find that there was a long line of cats waiting to get a turn. Hurricane sighed. It would be almost a half an hour before he could eat anything. He decided to go hunting so that he could get something for himself. He knew that if he waited in line to get food, not only would he be waiting forever, but by the time that he got his turn to grab something, it would either be down to all the old and bad food or completely empty.

Hurricane padded toward the crack in the wall. He emerged into a dark alley full of trashcans and dumpsters. The moon shone overhead, and a few wispy clouds dotted the sky. Jax and Link halted him once more.

"Halt," Jax demanded. "Where are you going?"

"Good one," Link said to him.

"Really?" Jax replied. "I've been practicing my 'halt'. I've also memorized the whole identification ordeal."

"Excellent, Jax."

"Are you training him to be an Entrance Guard?" Hurricane asked.

"Yes," Link answered. "I'm older, and Fletch ordered that I be his trainer."

"Good for you," Hurricane meowed. He began to leave.

"Hey!" Jax yowled after him. "You didn't answer my question!"

"More force in your voice, Jax," Hurricane heard Link say. "You need to make them understand that you're in charge."

"Okay, Link," Jax mewed, nodding.

Hurricane turned and walked back towards them. "Fine. Fire away."

Jax gave a little hop of excitement at his chance to impress Link with his Entrance Guard skills. "Tell us where you're going. It's important to know what each club cat is doing when they go outside of the club fort."

Link gave Jax a hard thud on his back. "Nice one."

Jax grinned.

"I'm going hunting, for your information."

Link nodded to signal Jax that he could proceed. "Are you bringing any trading items or valuable objects that should remain inside the club with you?"

Hurricane groaned. "What does it look like?"

"I'll tell you what it looks like," Jax said with force, shooting a quick glance at Link, waiting for some sign of approval. "It looks like that white sack around your neck is worthy of carrying something."

Hurricane suddenly flinched at the mention of the white Air Pouch. Who knows what could happen if they took it?

"I already told you. It's an old gift."

Link huffed.

Jax looked at Link. Link nodded. "Then you may proceed."

Hurricane let out a breath and left. He went to his favorite hunting spot, though it was quite far away. It was on the border of the city and the sparse forest. He could have gone to Central Park, but it was too popular there for stray cats.

He dove into a small bush after hearing the soft rustling of a rodent or bird. His mouth began watering as he imagined a juicy mouse for his dinner.

"Mmm..." he licked his lips.

After he caught what turned out to be a squirrel, he began heading back. But something made him stop. He heard a low rumbling laugh, and it made him want to drop the squirrel and bolt. But he didn't.

"Hurricane," a voice echoed, "Hurricane. Come to me, Hurricane."

Hurricane spun in circles. There was nobody there. "Hello? Show yourself!"

"Hurricane..." the voice came again. "Hurricane... Hurricane..."

The words bounced around in Hurricane's head. The voice echoed through the trees and grass. Everything whispered Hurricane's name. Every flower and every blade of grass. Every tree and every leaf.

Hurricane crouched on the ground and put his paws over his head. The squirrel fell down beside him. He grated his teeth and flattened his ears. *Too much noise, too much noise! I can't bear it all! My name is bouncing around in my head like a ping-pong ball!*

"Hurricane, Hurricane, Hurricane…"

"Stop! Please, stop!" Hurricane's head began to ache.

"Fine, Hurricane. I'll stop." The voice boomed from the trees and sky. Suddenly, everything went silent. Hurricane lifted his paws from his head. His blue eyes wildly scanned the area, but no one was to be seen.

Hurricane hissed. "Who are you? Why are you tormenting me?"

"I'm your worst nightmare."

A huge red and black shape swooped down from the sky on top of Hurricane. He screeched louder then ever before, and suddenly everything went black.

The last thing he saw were two blood-red eyes and the longest row of fangs he had ever seen.

Chapter 24

Three Days Later

Everest and Shade raced back to the abandoned house as fast as they could. Only one thing could have happened to Hurricane: he had been captured!

"I didn't think that they would start imprisoning so early in all this," Everest confessed.

"You said yourself that you highly doubted they would start imprisoning yet. You were wrong!" Shade gave Everest a hard nip on his side.

"Ow!" Everest barked. "Yes, I was wrong! And I'm sorry about that! But even the *best* Sighter Dogs can't tell *everything* that will happen in the future!"

Shade growled to himself in frustration. What would they do to Hurricane? Why did they capture him? *Did* they capture him?

Shade and Everest finally stopped at the steps of the abandoned house. Shade shuddered at the sight of it. He didn't feel safe here anymore. "I don't want to go in there."

"Neither do I. But we have to find out whether or not the Dark Forces have captured Hurricane. If not, we keep looking. If they did, we get him back."

"And what if they did?" Shade challenged. "They'll capture us, too. Who knows what will happen then."

"But imagine Hurricane. He's probably praying that we come save him. He must be terrified. What if that was you? Wouldn't *you* want to be rescued?"

Shade looked at his paws and brushed them against the sidewalk. "But still, I don't want to risk it…"

Everest's eye began blazing. "Shade, we don't have time to argue! Hurricane could be hurt, starving, or even dying as we speak! He's probably been tortured beyond belief. The Dark Forces don't have hearts. They don't care if someone dies under their claws. In fact, they relish the feeling of warm blood rushing through their talons. They *enjoy it.*"

Shade's eyes widened. The Dark Forces were heartless and cruel killers. They hid in the shadows, waiting for their chance to take an innocent soul. Little did people know that darkness was everywhere. In every hole, shadow, and around every corner. That was why Sighter Dogs even existed; to keep that darkness in its shadows and away from innocent lives. But Sighters sometimes can't keep darkness from creeping into someone's heart, and making them more horrible than they should be.

Shade nodded hesitantly. They had to save Hurricane.

Chapter 25

Present

"Let me go! Let me go!" Hurricane kicked at the sides of the rusted iron cage. He had woken up three days ago with his waist tied to a pole. His hind paws had been tied to the wooden floor, and his two front paws had been tied together at the wrists. They scored his arms with their claws multiple times, leaving stinging scar marks on them. It had only taken him a moment to realize that the Dark Forces had captured him. They had taken the Air Pouch to *who-knows*-where.

Beside him on another pole was something- well rather some*one*- that shocked him. It was the raven that he, Air, Shade, and Titus had fought. But this raven looked worse. His wings hung and his beak was crooked. Scars and cuts covered his whole body. Hurricane knew that they had left a few marks on him, but certainly not that many.

"What happened to you?" Hurricane asked. This raven had tried to *kill* him, but he still couldn't stand to see someone in that condition.

The raven eyed him angrily. His glare came with a threatening caw that was quickly cut off by a bout of coughing. "*You're* what happened, cat."

"I know we fought, but I know that I didn't do *that* much."

The raven looked at his two crooked wings. He sighed. "After failing to steal the Air Element from you, I was punished. The Dark Lord had wanted that element from becoming one of your collections. When I came back without it, he snapped. None of us could afford that loss."

Hurricane had suddenly felt a pang of regret. This raven had been doing his job. But at the same time, it was set on taking that element, and perhaps even killing for it.

"Around here, it doesn't matter who you are." The raven looked out the small window to his right. Clouds rolled past, and a few dull stars twinkled. The raven's eyes seemed to twinkle along with them. "Everyone is under command of the Dark Lord. If you're a higher rank, you get better treatment. Especially if you're part of the First Command." The raven turned his head back to Hurricane. "The First Command is the rank right next to the Dark Lord. If you're in the First Command, you get 'special treatment'."

"What Command Section are you in?" Hurricane asked. "Just out of curiosity."

"I'm in Ninth Command. It's next to last, which is Tenth Command."

"Oh."

"Every new recruit starts out in Tenth Command. They work their way up through the ranks until they're finally in First Command."

"Will you ever be the Dark Lord?" Hurricane questioned.

The raven shook his head. "Nobody will. Unless you're a dragon, that is. If you're a dragon, you have a chance."

"Why only dragons?"

The raven shrugged. "Tradition, I suppose."

"Are you a new recruit?"

"Sort of. I left the Tenth Command two years ago. Every year anyone in a rank below the First Command takes a test to see if they'll be promoted to a higher Command Section. Or sometimes if an individual does something amazing they're automatically recruited."

"I'm guessing you didn't pass last year and that's why you're still in Ninth Command?" Hurricane asked.

"Exactly. In fact, when I was trying to steal the Air Element, I was actually doing the yearly test. That's why I, of all the Dark Forces they could have chosen, was used."

Hurricane almost felt bad. He and the others had made this raven stay in the Ninth Command another year.

"Oh well. Three years in one Command Section can sometimes give you an advantage. When new recruits come in you get to show them around, and they're always listening to your every word since you know more."

"But at the same time they remain to treat you like trash."

The raven nodded. "You have a point, cat."

Hurricane cleared his throat and instinctively tried to hold out a paw to shake. Only then was he reminded that his arms were tied together. He pulled them back. "I'm Hurricane. I'm a stray."

The raven attempted to smile. But his eyes were dull and his expression was filled with pain and hunger. "I'm Banshee. I'm a raven of the Dark Forces."

"Is it true that Dark Forces hide around every corner and in every shadow?"

Banshee squinted his eyes in delight at a chance to scare someone. "Oh, we're not hiding. We're *waiting. Waiting* for a chance to pounce from our cover to terrify anyone we want."

Hurricane flattened his ears back in discomfort. "Um, okay…"

The raven laughed, coughing afterwards. He cringed as a few of his "disciplinary wounds" reopened. "I'll take that as a compliment. We Dark Forces creatures love the smell of fear."

The next day, an odd looking creature with huge fangs and long twisting horns and a short stubby tail had untied him. The monster swiped a claw down his side and it bled heavily. Hurricane yowled for someone to come and bandage him up. But nobody ever came. The creature threw him into a box-shaped rusted iron cage. Hurricane lay there all through the day, wailing for help and medical attention. When he first woke up tied to the pole, many creatures crowded around him to score a few claw marks into his fur. They all stung, and he wanted them mended. They hadn't even fed him anything but some murky brown water the second day he was there.

Now he lay in his cage, exhausted and starving. Hurricane wondered where Banshee had gone, and where *he* was, too.

Chapter 26

Present

Shade wiggled himself through the propped door. Everest had already squeezed through. Shade walked out onto the chilly wooden floor, shivering at the cold.

"Feels like autumn's shipping out and winter's taking its place." Shade let out a small *brrr*.

Everest huffed. "Yes, I suppose so. The Winter Solstice has almost arrived, and that means that the Sighter Dogs, *and* Sighter Cats will be meeting soon."

Shade looked up. The ceiling was a bleak gray color. So were all the walls. Everything was faded, shattered, broken, or tipped over. "Why do we meet here?"

Everest didn't answer. "I need to figure out a way for us to find Hurricane. Do you have any ideas, wolf?"

Shade turned, cocking his head. "Wolf? Is that a new nickname?"

"Just answer the question, Shade."

"Fine." Shade pinned back his ears, thinking hard. His tail slightly waved behind him as he thought. "I don't know. Could you zap us to the Rocky Mountains so we and other Sighters can put our heads together?"

Everest was about to answer when a low echoing laugh erupted all around them.

"Ha, ha, ha, ha…"

"I know that voice," Shade said with a snarl.

The laugh came again.

The fur along Everest's spine bristled. "Come out, Lord of Eternal Darkness!"

"Finally, someone who calls me by my proper name." A small vase with a dragon painting on it began shaking. Suddenly, the picture *spoke*.

"You both have quite a nerve for coming back to this place, don't you?" The dragon painting grinned as it criticized them. "What do I owe you now? More terror?"

Everest walked up to the vase. He lowered his head so that he would be face-to-face with the dragon painting. "I'll tell you what you owe us. Here's a hint: something with black fur, blue eyes, and a white pouch. Ring any bells, Dark Lord?"

The dragon in the painting suddenly turned from a mint green to red and black, the colors of the Lord of Darkness. "You got a small detail wrong, Everest." The dragon painting snapped its fingers. The Air Pouch was suddenly strung around his neck. "He doesn't carry the Air Pouch anymore."

Everest let out a howl of anger. He whacked the vase with a forepaw, sending it flying across the room to the couch. The dragon painting laughed with delight. "What a ride!"

"I'll shatter you to pieces next time." Everest's tail whipped angrily from side to side as his ears lay back against his head in frustration. His brow creased, and a growl rumbled from deep in his throat.

The painting got bigger, showing that it was getting closer to Everest's face. Shade stepped next to Everest. "Come now, Everest. No need to be impolite."

Everest snarled, leaning in closer to the vase. "You killed him, didn't you?"

The painting, or better known as the Dark Lord, laughed. "No need to jump to conclusions, dog. We Dark Forces creatures may love the feel of blood, but we don't kill everyone we meet." The Dark Lord's grin turned into a frown of disapproval. "Even if that someone is trying to get rid of you."

Everest growled. Shade stepped up to him. "Everest? Are...are you okay?"

Everest snarled. "What do you think, Half-mutt?"

107

Shade stepped backwards in horror. Everest *never* treated him like that. "You're not Everest."

"If I'm not Everest, who do you think I am?" Everest shook his head in confusion. "Oh, what's happening to me?"

Shade shoved the vase with his nose. "What did you do to him?"

The Dark Lord swung the Air Pouch in circles with a claw. "I did nothing."

"Yes you did!"

The Dark Lord threw the pouch in the air and caught it around his neck. "Well I suppose that I *may* have sent some vibes into the air," he grinned even wider, "by mistake."

"You did it on purpose! You're turning Everest into one of you!" Shade jumped onto the couch and kicked the vase with his back paws. The vase went tumbling onto the floor with a piercing crash. Dozens of pieces of glass glinted on the wooden floor.

The pieces that had parts of the dragon painting went completely still. But they didn't turn green as they were before. They stayed the colors of the Dark Lord, black and red.

Suddenly, the pieces with parts of the dragon on them turned white like the rest of the vase as the dragon painting seeped out onto the floor. The painting came back together as it slithered across the old wood towards the gray wall. When it finally reached the wall, it grew as tall as it would allow. Now the painting was on the wall.

"You just won't go away, will you?" Shade growled.

Everest pawed at the floor. "You must be too scared to face us, so you decide to stay a painting, right?"

The Dark Lord knocked down a framed photo that was in his way. "No, actually. In my real form, I'm *far* too large to fit in this room. My head would go through the ceiling."

Shade was done stalling. "Tell us where Hurricane is!"

The Dark Lord howled with laughter. "You really think that I would just *tell* you where he is? Oh Shade, you crack me up!"

108

Shade's claws scored the floor. "Tell us!"

The Dark Lord turned to them once more. "I refuse to tell you. But I will tell you this riddle."

Shade moaned. "A riddle? How original."

"Fire away," Everest growled.

"Gladly," the Dark Lord answered. "Ahem. *A place you must find is far, far away. The rules are to find it right now, today. But you first must collect a thing of great power. It's wet, it's clear, and it nourishes flowers. This element is strong, so you must find it quick. But be careful of things that bump, growl and click. I've set up traps, be careful where you step. I wish you* little *luck on your rescuing quest.*"

Shade cocked his head. "Traps? A wet element? Things that bump growl and click? I don't get it."

"Figure it out soon, because I'm sending you on your quest."

"Explain to us about this quest."

The Dark Lord twirled his staff. "Fine, then. You will begin your quest at a certain starting point. From there you must travel through thick and thin to find a 'wet element'. If you can find the element, then I will release Hurricane. If not... well, you'll see."

Shade nodded. "Alright. You have a deal."

The Dark Lord grinned devilishly. "Excellent."

A red haze clouded Shade's vision. Suddenly, there was nothing left but, once again, a rich crimson.

Chapter 27

When the red haze cleared, Shade found himself in the midst of a dense forest. Vines hung from every tree, bushes and undergrowth hid the lush grass beneath.

Well, it looks like I'll be finding this element without Hurricane for the first time. Shade looked to his side, finding that Everest was standing there. *And instead, with the dog that usually* sends *us on the quests.*

"Well, come on Everest. We've got a ways to go."

Everest bristled a bit. "Okay, but... Shade? I don't really feel like myself."

"What do you mean?" Shade asked, concerned.

Everest pinned back his ears and bristled some more. "I feel very..." Everest started growling, "dangerous."

"Dangerous?" Shade stepped back. "What do you mean, 'dangerous'?"

"I just feel like I'm about to snap. You might want to be careful around me, Shade. I think it might have to do with what the Dark Lord said when he told us that he put out some 'vibes'. I think that those vibes are gradually making me more like a Dark Force creature."

Shade trembled. "So, you might turn against me?"

Everest shrugged. "I don't know, Shade. Just... don't entirely trust everything I say. I don't know if that's the problem, maybe I'm just feverish, but still."

Shade nodded. "Okay."

Suddenly, they heard the Dark Lord's voice echo around them once more. "*Ha, ha, ha, ha...*"

Everest crouched low to the ground, stiffening his tail. All the fur on his body bristled as a threatening growl rumbled in his throat. "What do you want with us, dragon?"

"*Oh, I'm only here to give you two a few tips. This first one is for you, Shade.*"

Shade pinned back his ears, growling quietly.

"*Everest will gradually become more and more untrustworthy throughout your quest. His dangerous state will only become more significant as the journey progresses. It is a slow processing spell I've cast upon him. Though, for now, you can entirely trust him. But don't become too comfortable. He will turn against you soon.*"

Everest's eyes widened in terror.

"Show yourself, Dark Lord!"

"*I'm afraid that I can't do that, Shade. Though I will guide you through your quest by speaking through your minds.*"

Shade snarled in reply.

"*This next bit of information is for you, Everest. As you begin to turn nefarious, you will feel intense anger and frustration.*"

Everest nodded hesitantly. His one good blue eye glittered with the beginnings of the symptoms.

Shade turned to begin walking. Everest followed.

"*As the riddle goes, you two: 'I wish you little luck on your rescuing quest'! Little luck!*"

Shade flicked an ear and whipped his tail once before engulfing himself in the dark green of the growth.

Chapter 28

Shade crawled through a long line of shrubs. Sticks and twigs got caught in his fur. He heard Everest's claws clicking each time his paw hit a branch.

Clicking…

Maybe that's what the Dark Lord meant by things that bump, growl and click. 'But be careful of things that bump growl and click'. I have to be careful of Everest?

Shade nudged Everest with his nose. "How do you feel?"

The second Shade's nose touched Everest's ear, Everest whirled around and snapped at Shade with his thorn-sharp fangs. Shade jumped out of the way just in time.

Everest let out a low threatening growl. "Don't touch me." Angrily, he began stalking toward Shade, oblivious to the twigs that scraped his legs.

"Everest! Calm down!" Shade backed up more and more as Everest came closer. Suddenly Shade tried something. Shade grabbed a stick in his mouth and whacked Everest across his black eye patch. Everest cried out, lying down to put a paw over his bad eye.

Everest looked up at Shade. His good eye twinkled with a mixture of anger and terror. "I'm fine. Let's keep going."

As the two kept walking, the same dastardly voice rang in their heads. "*This is the first level of testing. Before you actually start your journey, I would like to have a better outlook on how you will do. This test is to see how well you will do in going through dense forest life. I really hope you can cope with this because the fun has only just begun.*"

"The fun?" Shade growled.

"Sorry to break it to you Oh Lord of Eternal Darkness, but, there isn't exactly any fun in this."

The two of them heard the Dark Lord laugh with contentment. "*Well it is for me! Just to see the pathetic looks on your faces is really quite enjoyable.*"

"Wow, thanks," Shade said sarcastically.

"You're quite welcome, Shade," the Dark Lord said laughing. *"Well, this chit-chat is really quite fun but I believe that I must be going. But don't worry; I'll be watching you the whole way."*

Shade turned to Everest as the voice left their heads. "Okay. So, let's try deciphering this riddle. What does the Dark Lord mean by a wet element?"

"He must mean the next element, the third one. It's either Water or Fire, since we've already collected Earth and Air. Fire can't get wet or it will be put out, so the next element must be Water."

"Good. So I'm guessing that the color of the globe that it is in will be blue?"

"I suppose so," Everest answered. "Water is wet, clear, and flowers need it to grow. So that's what we're looking for." Everest bristled a bit more, but forced his fur to lay flat.

Shade nodded. "Let's go."

*   *   *   *   *   *   *   *   *

After about a half an hour of dragging their paws through shrubs, the two came into a clearing. The clearing was a small, circular-shaped patch of grass that opened up in the middle of the forest.

Shade looked at Everest. Everest shrugged. "I guess that we just keep walking."

Everest nodded. The two got about halfway through the clearing when the voice telepathically came once more.

"Stop, this is another test."

Shade looked all around for the familiar beady red eyes. The Dark Lord was nowhere in sight. "Fine. What's the next test?"

"One of my companions will be taking you both on. You may recognize him."

Shade and Everest whirled in all directions. There was nobody that they could see.

"Here he comes now."

A shadow fell over them. Something was blocking the sun from the sky. When they looked up, they were surprised to see yet another raven. When the raven landed in front of them, they immediately recognized him. It was the raven they had fought for the Air Element!

The raven looked at them in pure hatred for the scars that they had given it. Shade remembered how Air, the white winged she-cat with silver swirling patterns, had helped to defeat it, and how it had almost captured Titus, the German Shepherd pup who had been their guide to the second element. They had defeated the raven that time, but now they weren't so sure. There had been four of them that time, including Hurricane, but now it was just Shade and Everest. Everest wasn't even there the last time.

Shade snarled at the raven. "Step back or we'll leave more scars on you than before."

The raven cawed threateningly. "Oh, no. This time you will feel the regret of defeat."

Chapter 29

One Hour Earlier

Hurricane lay on his stomach, starving. No food, no water. Only on the second day that he was there had he gotten a small bowl of murky water. Otherwise, he had been given nothing.

"Help... me... I need-" Hurricane coughed, "food. My mouth is so dry. Please, please, *please* let me have a drink of water..." Hurricane meowed these words even though nobody was there. Not even a sentry guard to make sure he didn't escape the cell. If he did, the door was metal and had a padlock. The window had seemed like a chance, but all that there was were clouds. He considered that they were up in the sky. It seemed impossible, but these were Dark Forces creatures. They could do just about anything, including having a fortified settlement in the clouds.

Hurricane yowled again. No one came.

An hour passed. Two hours. Three. No food and no water all the while. Finally, Hurricane heard the padlock being unlocked. He lifted his head. Moving made his cuts sting and his muscles ache. "Hello?"

A werewolf-looking creature walked in on two legs. "The Dark Lord is here to speak with you."

A huge head came through the door. "Hello, Hurricane. I'd love to come in and sit but I'm far too big for this little chamber."

Hurricane moaned in pain. "Food..."

The Dark Lord made a sarcastic look of disapproval. "Oh, of course! Ratri, go get this poor tom something good to eat. Lots of protein, not to mention a big bowl of crystal-clear water."

Hurricane moaned again. "Food..."

"Yes, yes. Your food is coming."

Hurricane coughed.

"I'm truly sorry about your condition, Hurricane. I am *appalled* by how my men have treated our guest."

"You're not upset." Hurricane coughed again. "You're completely overjoyed."

The dragon blew a bit of smoke. "Oh well. Think what you want, cat. Allow me to explain why I came to this dreaded cell. I would like to inform you that I am about to send your little friends, Shade and Everest, on a quest to save you."

"A quest?" Hurricane rolled from his side to his stomach. His head hung. "What do you mean?"

The werewolf creature came back, holding a bowl of water and a baked chicken. "Here you go. It's clear water and high protein. Enjoy." He handed the food over to the Dark Lord.

"Thank you, Ratri." The Dark Lord nodded to Ratri, the werewolf, and it left. "Here you are, Hurricane." The Dark Lord opened the cell door to set down the food.

Hurricane saw his chance. But the food smelled so good, and he could barely lift himself up anyway.

"I can see your eyes twinkling at the opportunity, Hurricane, but," the Dark Lord closed the cell with a loud bang, "it's not a good idea. Trust me."

Hurricane heaved himself up. He literally face-planted into the water. It felt so good in the steamy chamber. He opened his mouth and let the cool, clear water flow in. He lay with his entire face in the bowl for a while. His ears weren't under, so he could still hear.

"I've made a deal with them. If they can find the next element, I will release you. If not, I'll keep you here permanently."

"Your last line of defense was pretty weak, Dark Lord," Hurricane growled, lifting his sopping wet head from the bowl.

"Sending the raven was a mistake on my part and the First Command's part. The First Command is - -"

"Banshee already explained about the Command Sections, Dark Lord."

"The raven? He told you his name? Oh, of course. It's efficient that I don't have to explain Command Sections to someone of your kind."

"One of my kind? Is that some sort of insult, dragon?"

"By that I mean... one that isn't of the Dark Forces."

"I see." Hurricane answered, pinning back his ears.

"Eat. Drink. Enjoy your meal. I have important Lord of Eternal Darkness duties to attend to."

"Gladly." Hurricane began digging into the chicken, greedily gnawing on a leg.

The Dark Lord left Hurricane to his feast. Nothing had ever tasted so good. The chicken filled his belly. He purred with delight. Hurricane lapped up as much of the water that he could hold and wallowed in what was left. The cold water soothed the cuts and his aching muscles and pads.

Hurricane curled up in the bowl. Water sloshed out of it, but he didn't care. It felt wonderful. He was about to drift off into a nap when the Dark Lord came back in. Hurricane twitched his nose and whiskers while lifting up his head. His eyelids drooped.

"And Hurricane," the Dark Lord began, "If you prefer, call me by my name before I became the Dark Lord: Than. Do you know what Than means?"

Hurricane coughed. "What?"

"It means 'death'."

Chapter 30

Present

"Alright. I've fought you before. I can fight you again. You look even scrawnier than before, anyway." Shade crouched down and backed up, preparing to leap at the raven. "But you can talk this time."

"I could always talk. I was just too busy fighting to be held up with any chitchat, and besides, to whom did I have to speak? I was the only Dark Force out there." The raven clawed at the grass with his razor sharp talons, leaving three lines of dirt in the lush green.

Everest bristled again, forcing down the urge to turn on Shade. "Shade, it's getting harder to control."

"Just keep trying." Shade turned his head to the Sighter Dog. "Think about Hurricane. If you don't control the spell, then we'll never save him."

Everest nodded.

Shade turned his head back to the raven. "You may as well tell us your name this time, bird."

"It's Banshee. Screaming Banshee. But you can just call me Banshee. Want to know what I do best?"

Shade creased his brow. "What?"

The raven suddenly looked to one side as though something had caught his eye. Shade and Everest looked in the same direction. There was nothing there. When they looked back at the raven, he was gone.

They heard a voice behind them. "I can vanish. Like a ghost."

They whipped around and leaped at Banshee. "No, you can just move really fast!" Shade barked, biting a wing. The raven turned around and snapped at Everest's leg with its beak. Everest howled in pain, swiping a paw across the raven's face. His claws left four scars down the middle of his face. The raven got back at him by scoring its talons down Everest's side. He limped to the other side of the clearing, feeling far too much pain to move. He flopped down by a small boulder.

"Everest!" Shade barked. "The battle has only just begun! I need help!"

Everest groaned. "I can't move... the talons... I'm bleeding... bleeding out..."

Shade roared in anger. He leaped on the back of the raven and clamped down hard on his neck. Banshee screeched in pain, and fell to the ground. He began lifting off, but Shade wasn't finished. He bit down hard on the right wing, which was left with bleeding fang-marks. As Shade began to leap off of the raven, he caught him with his talons on Shade's right flank. Shade yelped. He bolted to the edge of the clearing where Everest lay. The raven lifted into the sky flapping twice with his right wing for every one flap of his left wing.

"Everest? Are you all right?" Shade looked up just as the raven was diving for them one last time. It clawed Shade down his back, making him cry out louder than ever before. Shade spun around, blocking Everest from the Banshee. Shade made a warning bite on the raven's leg, signaling for Banshee to leave. Banshee cawed in anger, and left.

"Everest? Everest, are you alright?"

Everest moaned. "I think so."

"Can you stand?"

Everest heaved himself up with a groan of protest. "Yes."

"Can you walk?"

Everest took a step. Then he attempted to walk to the other side of the clearing. "Yes, I can."

"Do you think you can make the rest of the journey?"

"I think I can. I'll force myself to."

"Don't do that."

"Shade, we have to save Hurricane. I'm coming."

Shade nodded hesitantly. He and Everest needed to stick together.

119

Chapter 31

Everest wouldn't stop bleeding. The long slash across his side was too deep and too long. Everest kept repeating that they stung. Shade kept saying that he understood.

"They sting and I can barely feel my side," Everest complained.

"I know," Shade kept patiently answering. "I know."

"*Congratulations you two, you have officially completed the second test.*"

Shade didn't even flick an ear at the voice this time.

"*I believe that you both could use a nice, steady, cooling run. Oops, did I say 'cooling run'? I meant race for your lives.*"

Shade's head flew up. "What?"

"*Everyone loves a thrilling race, now don't they?*"

Shade and Everest began walking faster. "What are we racing? Tell us what we're racing!"

"*This is your third and final test. I'm going to clock your speed, and see if you have strong legs. Strong enough legs for you to save your own lives.*" A noise like thunder gradually got louder in the background.

Shade pinned back his ears and began jogging. "What are we racing?" He yelped. The noise was becoming so loud that they had to yell.

The Dark Lord simply said, "*Bison.*"

"Bison?" Shade's voice was immediately lost as a huge herd of snorting, thundering, roaring bison burst through the trees. Shade howled into the sunset sky, knowing it was his last.

Suddenly, something grabbed him by the scruff and yanked him forward. When Shade turned to see what or who it was, Everest was clinging to his scruff. Shade and Everest began running for their lives once Everest let go.

Everest and Shade galloped through the dense woods. They couldn't go left or right because of how tightly packed the trees were. The bison were roaring in an uncontrollable rage that caused them to pursue the two dogs. Though perhaps lasting only several minutes, the race seemed to last for hours. Shade's legs ached from the long run, and he didn't know how much longer he could keep this up. Everest looked as though he were about to drop to the ground.

That's when they saw the tail. A small orange and black striped tail hung from the canopies above their heads. The tail seemed to be following them as they ran. Shade barely gave the tail a second thought. All his interest in anything had been drained out of him by the long run. His legs felt as though they were about to fall off. He kept coughing because of how quickly he was forced to draw in breaths.

Just as Shade was considering giving up and dropping, something amazing happened.

A young tiger cub with a long twisty tail and bright amber eyes fell from the trees in front of the bison. He let out a shrill roar. When nothing happened, he drew in a deep breath. Shade, Everest, and the bison were about to trample him. But when Shade saw the tiger, he only ran faster. A bison stampede, and a tiger? He had to get away. But then the tiger cub did something miraculous. He lifted his head after the breath he took and let out a huge roar for his size. The bison stopped in their tracks and reared up, giving the tiger cub enough time to motion to an opening in the tree trunks just big enough for Shade and Everest to squeeze through.

Shade spun to his left side and disappeared into the trunks, Everest close behind. When he turned to look out through the space, the bison were beginning to run again. The tiger cub stood boldly in their path, grinning. Just as the lead bison was about to run him over, the tiger cub leaped up and grabbed a low hanging branch. For a few moments, he hung there, waiting for the bison stampede to leave.

Once they were all gone, aside from a few stragglers who were starting to leave as well, the cub began curling up his back legs toward the branch that he was clinging to. Once his back paws reached the branch, he sunk his claws into the wood. He then turned himself upright on the branch and climbed into the trees. For a moment there was silence, aside from some rustling in the trees and a fading echo of thundering hooves. Then the tiger cub dropped down behind the two dogs, making them jump.

"Hi!" he mewed happily. "I'm Jay. I saved you!"

Shade and Everest nodded their thanks, too tired to speak. They both flopped down on the ground, panting.

"You should have seen me! I was running through the trees, leaping across branches and through leaves, and the whole time I made sure that my tail hung down so that you could see it! Wasn't that clever? Then I let myself fall from the trees and I roared! I really roared! I've never felt so alive!"

Shade and Everest sighed their replies.

"Oh, you're probably tired and thirsty."

Shade flicked an ear, his eyes brightening at the thought of water.

"I know where some water is, if you would like for me to fetch some for you."

Shade's head popped up. "Yes, please! That would be wonderful… Jay, is it?"

"Yep!" piped Jay.

"Thank you. Please, bring enough for both of us."

Everest started snoring softly. He had fallen asleep.

"You've got it, Shade!"

Shade cocked his head. "You know my name?"

"Yeah. I also know that he's Everest, a Sighter Dog, and that you're both trying to save Hurricane the cat from the Dark Forces." Jay turned to leave.

"How?" Shade asked.

Jay laughed. "I'm your guide, silly." He left through the space.

Shade smiled. A tiger for their guide was quite an interesting change.

Chapter 32

Shade dreamed of water rushing down a crisp waterfall. It was clear and beautiful to watch. The sunset over the water made it gleam with different shades of orange and yellow. Finally, the color turned to red. But the red wasn't coming from the sunset. The *water* had turned red. The pool that the red water was flowing into turned crimson as well, and then it began to overflow. Shade backed up to avoid touching the red water. But it kept flowing onto land so much faster and faster that Shade began running from it. At one point, he came to a dead end. A jagged wall of stone and rock loomed in front of him, blocking the exit. The red water began covering Shade's paws. But then he realized that it wasn't water. It was *blood.*

The blood was rising up to Shade's belly. He stared wildly around. When he looked up, he saw Everest on the ledge of the rock wall. "Everest! Help me!"

"Shade!" Everest barked. Everest held out a paw. Shade tried to grab it with his teeth. Just as he was about to grab hold of Everest's paw, he retracted it. Shade's back was almost all the way under now. "Everest! Help!" Everest didn't respond, but he grinned menacingly. Everest's eyes began to collect a red haze. His claws glinted in the setting sun, making them look longer. Beneath his eye patch, a red glow began shining as well. He laughed, then turned around and left.

"Everest! Come back!" The blood had covered Shade's neck completely. He had to hold his head high above the blood. "Help! Somebody! Help me!"

Then the Dark Lord's head appeared over the ledge. "You're doomed to die, Shade. Just give up, won't you? The Dark Lord grabbed the Earth Pouch from around Shade's neck.

"Give that back!" Shade snapped at the Dark Lord's claw. He missed by an inch.

"Oh, too bad. Looks like the lil' doggie has been defeated for once." The Dark Lord leaned into Shade's face. "Does that make the lil' doggie sad?"

Suddenly the Air Pouch appeared in the Dark Lord's other claw. "Oh, won't you look at that? Seems as though somebody lost this little trinket, eh?"

Shade began writhing madly at the sight of the Air Pouch. "Where did you get that?"

"Just from a little friend of yours. I must say, he was very cooperative when he was tied to a pole."

"You tied up Hurricane?"

"First, I knocked him unconscious. We tied him to a pole in his state of unknowing, and when he woke up, every Dark Force creature in the First Command got a turn at putting a wound on him. Then, we threw him into a jail cell, which was quite a bit more comfortable."

Shade snarled at the Dark Lord. "You heartless beast! Every Dark Force creature in the First Command? What kind of sick idiot are you?"

"I'm a dragon, for your information." The Dark Lord snapped his fingers. The blood began overflowing faster than ever to the point that it covered Shade's head. He tried swimming frantically upwards, but the blood was so sticky that it held him. He began to panic. His heart beat faster and faster as the blood held him. His lungs were screaming for air. His vision began fading, his heart slowing...

*   *   *   *   *   *   *   *   *

Shade woke with a gasp. He coughed and coughed while breathing deep breaths of the cool, fresh air. Inhaling and exhaling had never felt so wonderful. "Oh... my God..."

Everest turned to Shade from his spot. "Shade? Is something wrong?"

Shade leaped to his paws. He backed away from Everest. "Don't touch me. Get away!"

Everest pinned back his ears then stood up. He lowered his head to show that he wasn't a threat. "Shade? Calm down. What's wrong?"

"A dream... b-blood and I needed air and... and... the Dark Lord and you left and-"

"Shade! *Slow down.* Tell me what happened."

Shade coughed and sat on his haunches. He breathed another refreshing breath. His heart was beating faster than a racehorse. "I had a dream that I was watching a waterfall. The falls turned red and I ran away from it as it began to overflow. Then I came to this big wall of stone and I was trapped. The red water turned out to be blood. The blood was starting to cover me and then I saw you on the ledge. You reached a paw towards me, and as I was about to grab it, you pulled it away. Then this evil expression came over your face and you left. I started barking for you to come back when the Dark Lord appeared on the ledge." Shade took a breath. "He stole my Earth Pouch and told me that they had tortured Hurricane then put him in a cell. Then he snapped his fingers and the blood covered me. I tried swimming to the top, but I couldn't. I couldn't breath. My vision started to go and then I woke up."

Everest nodded. "I think that the dream foreshadows what's ahead." Everest bristled. "The waterfall could stand for a steady, easily flowing life, but when the water turned red, it might have meant war, or death. The ledge probably meant that the enemy is stronger than we think, and when I left you there..." Everest trailed off.

"It was reminding us of the fact that the spell over you is getting stronger as time passes, and that if we don't find the Water Element soon, you'll turn over to the Dark Forces."

Everest lowered his head in shame. "Yes. But again with the dream: you said that the Dark Lord appeared?"

"Yeah. He told me about how they were treating Hurricane with torture."

"Then when he snapped his fingers and drowned you, he was trying to convince us that we should give up."

"Well, we can't! Hurricane needs us!" Shade was cut off by a bout of coughing.

"Settle down, Shade. We both want to find Hurricane. But it's important that you save your strength. Jay will be back with water for us in a few-"

"Seconds!" a voice mewed. There was Jay, holding two old bottles filled with water. "Here you go! Fresh, clean, and straight from the spring! I always collect little doodads that I find, like these bottles, in case I ever need them."

"Where do you put all of it?"

"In my den."

"Oh... your den? You have a den?"

"Yep! It's in the hole of this *huge* oak tree on the other side of the path where you two were about to get trampled!"

Shade nodded. "Do you mind if you take us there?"

"Um... okay. But drink that water first! It's important." Jay shoved the water forward.

Shade and Everest drank as much as they could hold, and then followed Jay across the path.

"I can't wait for you to see it. It's a really great place! I have all sorts of doodads and knick-knacks in there." Jay halted in front of one of the biggest trees that Shade had ever seen. "Here we are!"

"Wow," breathed Shade. "It's huge."

"I know! Come on in!" Jay disappeared among the twisted roots. Shade and Everest followed close behind.

It took a moment for Shade's eyes to adjust to the dim light. Jay jumped up towards a few leaves that covered a section of the inside of the trunk. "Too dark? Sorry." Jay shoved away the leaves. A small hole appeared, and rays of beautiful sunlight shown through. "I call it my window!"

Shade could see now. Jay had knocked a few dents in the wall where he stored dozens of items. There were toys, silverware, weapons, handkerchiefs, blankets, towels, and more. On the ground, he had rolled out an old carpet. A pillow and a blanket were placed neatly in the corner. "That's my bed," Jay pointed out.

Shade marveled at all of Jay's things. There was so much. "Where do you find all of this stuff?"

"It's just left behind by Dark Forces sometimes. They travel through here every now and then and drop stuff."

"They must be pretty clumsy." Shade pulled out a bandana. It was red with black dots. "Do you mind if I try this on?"

"Sure," said Jay. "Help yourself."

Shade stood there. "Um, could you put it on, please?"

"Oh, yeah! Of course." Jay took the bandana in his mouth and jumped on Shade's back. Shade winced.

"Retract the claws, please. Ouch!"

"Oh! Sorry." Jay tied the bandana around Shade's neck and jumped down. "There!"

Shade looked down. The bandana covered the Earth Pouch. His plan had worked. "Do you mind if I keep this?"

Jay tilted his head. "Well, if you want one, I think a blue bandana would work better." Jay walked back over to his "shelves". He pulled out a bright blue bandana with red swirls. He tied it around Shade's neck and put the red one back. He turned and looked at Shade. "Just as I thought. Much better!"

Shade smiled. His plan was to keep the Earth Pouch hidden from Dark Forces creatures, or other strays like Snag and his gang.

Shade dipped his head to Jay. "Thank you."

Jay gave a little bounce.

Everest stepped between the two of them "Sorry to interrupt. But shouldn't we be going?" Everest bristled even more this time.

Shade nodded. "Yeah. Come on."

"*Yes. You had better get moving. I'm growing very bored watching you sleep and drink and talk.*"

Shade growled at the voice. But for some reason, Everest didn't.

"*You've gone through your tests and passed with flying colors. Your little guide here will show you to the Water Element.*"

Jay crouched down. "Um, okay. Come on, guys." Jay padded out through the crack in the trunk. Shade and Everest followed.

Shade fell in step beside Everest. "Everest? Are you feeling okay?"

Everest said nothing. His only reply was a slight growling noise deep in his throat. His eyes seemed to flash an emotion that Shade couldn't place. Was it anger? Or perhaps hatred?

"Everest?"

Everest whipped his head around. "I feel fine you idiot!"

Shade bolted forward and walked next to Jay. Shade shook his head as he looked at Everest's bristling form. "He's losing it."

Jay nodded. "The spell is getting stronger."

Shade lowered his head so that it was level with Jay's. "You know about the spell?"

Jay grinned. "Here's a little trivia for you about us guides: we're filled in about everything before we start guiding you guys."

Shade smiled. "Alright then."

After a few minutes, the path opened up to a huge arena. It was completely bare, and there were boulders surrounding the dusty clearing. In the center, the Water Element was levitating in its globe. Shade bounded forward, but then stopped himself. There had to be a reason that the element was in an *arena* of all places.

"*Well? What are you waiting for? Go ahead.*"

"No," Shade declared. "Not until we know what we have to do."

The Dark Lord sighed. "*Don't you like surprises though?*"

"Not when they're from you."

"*Alright then. Prepare for a little something… unexpected.*" Shade heard the Dark Lord snap his fingers.

Suddenly, something terrible happened. *Everest* leaped at Shade and knocked him to the ground.

"Prepare to die, you pest."

Chapter 33

Shade writhed under Everest's grasp. Everest clamped his fangs down hard on Shade's neck, his good eye glowing with anger and insanity. "Everest!" Shade coughed. "Everest, stop!"

Everest growled deep in his throat and clamped down harder.

Shade coughed and hacked while trying to get a hold on Everest with his paws. His hind legs flailed wildly, and he was finally able to muster up enough strength to kick Everest off. Everest fell onto his side about two feet from Shade and leapt to his paws. Shade stood in shock right in front of him. Jay leapt at Everest from behind, claws outstretched and yowling. Everest turned around just as Jay sunk his claws deep into his flank, and he let out a yelp of pain. Shade shook his head and bounded toward Everest's face. He bit down hard on Everest's snout, keeping it shut as Jay reopened the wound that Banshee had made with his talons, and also leaving a few marks of his own.

Everest spun around so fast that he fell to the ground. Shade momentarily let go of Everest's snout to make a v-shaped cut in his ear. Everest howled and barked and yelped and screeched, until he was finally able to shake free.

The Dark Lord appeared, standing on a huge boulder that was among the ones surrounding the clearing to make an arena. He tossed the Air Pouch from claw to claw and set his staff down next to him. He lay down to get more comfortable. "My, this is exciting. Make a move, Shade. He'll get away."

Shade barked angrily at the Dark Lord before Everest knocked him to the ground once more. He let out a yelp of surprise. Everest was about to bite Shade's neck again when Jay jumped at his face, giving Shade time to slip away. Jay batted at Everest's head with his claws unsheathed. He left scars along his face, and his eye-patch fell off.

Shade cringed as Everest roared in anger. A scar ran down his eye, which was permanently closed. There was fur, but it was shorter than the rest on his face. Shade backed away.

Everest stopped running. He halted in front of his eye-patch. He looked defeated. He hung his head.

The Dark Lord walked forward and shoved at Everest's head with his staff. "Fight them!"

Everest stood still for a moment. Suddenly, he leapt at Jay. For one split second, Shade thought he would run to Jay's defense, but he had a better idea. He ran towards the Water Element and grabbed it. "Water, the third element." A blue pouch appeared around his neck. The globe dropped into his paws.

The Dark Lord whirled around. "No!"

Shade pressed against both sides. A teardrop shaped portion of water fell into his paws. Everest let go of Jay and slowly stepped backwards. He fell to the ground. Shade took the teardrop shaped portion in his teeth.

The Dark Lord flapped his wings and began to fly towards him. "Don't!"

A wave of water rose up out of the dust. When it cleared, a blue wolf stood in its place. She howled into the sunset sky, and another wave pushed the Dark Lord back.

"Who are you?" barked Shade through his teeth and over the sound of roaring waves. The blue wolf turned to face him. Her sea-blue eyes put him at ease.

"I am Water, keeper of the third element." She turned to the Dark Lord. "They have played your little game, Lord of Darkness. Release Hurricane!"

The Dark Lord coughed and sputtered. "Never!"

Water directed another blast of water at him.

"No! I won't let him free!"

"Then I will drown you!" Water howled louder than ever before. Shade heard the roar of a wave in the distance.

"No! You can't drown me! I am the Dark Lord!"

"I can, and I will!"

"Please! Stop! I'll set him free, I'll set him free!"

The roaring ceased. "Then do so."

The Dark Lord snapped his fingers with one claw, and with the other, he pointed his staff into the air. A loud bang erupted through the twilight.

A blue blast sent them all tumbling backwards. When they looked up, Hurricane was standing there!

"Hurricane!" They shouted over and over. Hurricane stumbled in Shade's direction.

"Shade!" he exclaimed weakly. "I'm free!"

Shade crouched low and supported Hurricane. "Are you alright?"

Hurricane gave a weak laugh. "Shade, I've been through a lot. You think that a lack of food is going to do anything to me?"

"But you aren't just starved. You're injured!"

Hurricane looked down at himself. "Yeah, well, what do you expect if you're getting captured by the Dark Forces, huh?"

Shade nodded, and then boosted Hurricane onto his back. Hurricane lay there, breathing slowly. "Water? Can you help him?"

Water pinned back her ears. "I'll try." She walked towards Hurricane.

He coughed and looked at her with a bit of interest. "Are you the keeper of the-" he coughed, "the third element?"

"Yes," Water answered. She leaned toward Hurricane's head and started whispering words that were too soft to hear. Hurricane's eyes began to close.

Hurricane's eyes suddenly shot open. His ice-blue irises cast a glow that lit up Shade's black and gray fur. As his eyes shone, Water kept whispering words, and his wounds began to slowly disappear. Finally, they were completely gone. Hurricane looked at his jet-black fur. His pelt shimmered like dozens of stars. A light went back into his sky-colored eyes.

"Thank you," he sighed.

131

"You're welcome, Hurricane," Water replied.

Jay limped over to Shade. "Let's put the water into the Water Pouch." Jay took the water from Shade and opened the pouch. He dropped it in and closed it. The embroidered "W" began glowing gold.

Water marched over to where the Dark Lord perched, scowling. "Hand over the Air Pouch," she ordered.

The Dark Lord growled and held it out. Water took it and set it on the ground to look inside. The Air Element was still there. She sighed with relief. She picked it up once more and asked for Jay to tie it around Hurricane's neck. Jay nodded and took the pouch in his mouth. He then went over to Hurricane and tied it around his neck. Hurricane curled onto Shade's back.

"What say I carry you home?" Shade asked.

Hurricane laughed. "Yeah."

"We're ready, Water-"

"Wait!" Jay mewed. "Everest is hurt!"

They all turned to Everest. He lay on the ground, moaning. His eye-patch was about a foot away from him.

Hurricane lifted his head and saw Everest's face. He cringed at the scar. "Well, at least there's still fur and it's not completely bare there."

Everest hid his head.

They all, aside from the Dark Lord who disappeared, walked timidly over to Everest. "Leave me alone."

"No," said Shade simply. He nodded to Jay who quickly tied Everest's eye-patch back on.

Everest looked around at the crowd. They all stood silently, waiting for him to pounce at one of them. But he just lay there.

Suddenly, he shook his head. "I'm sorry, Shade. I'm sorry, Jay. But I think that the spell is gone."

Shade nodded, smiling. "You never told us that you could fight, Everest!"

Everest smiled. "I'm a Sighter Dog. Our job is to protect the planet. You don't think that I wouldn't have a few tricks up my sleeve, do you?"

They all laughed.

Water nudged Shade. "Time to go." She backed up. Jay ran over to her and sat down. "Goodbye!" she said sweetly.

Shade smiled even more. "Goodbye!" He touched his nose to Jay's, and then Water's.

"You fought bravely today, Shade," she complimented.

"Thank you, and you did too," he replied.

She smiled, and her eyes twinkled with beauty.

A blue light tore Shade away from Water, and sent them all back to the abandoned house. Shade stood there for a bit, trying to keep the moment a little longer, until Everest began speaking.

"Wow," he began, "That was amazing. After we left Jay's den, I actually thought that I was a Dark Force creature."

Shade shook his head. He turned to Everest. "Yeah. Yes, of course."

"Are you okay?" Shade heard Hurricane on his back.

"Yeah, I'm fine. Um, you can get down now." Hurricane did as he was told and leapt off of Shade.

"I need to get going," Hurricane declared. "I've been gone for three days, so Fletch will want a good excuse. Lexie must be terrified."

Shade nodded, and Hurricane slipped out. Everest turned to Shade. "You're sure you're okay?"

"I'm fine, it's just... a lot to take in."

Everest flicked an ear. "I know how you feel. Well, you'd best be getting home, Shade."

Shade flicked his tail. "Okay. Bye, Everest."

133

Everest smiled, and disappeared. Shade walked down the sidewalk to his cool and shadowed alley, where he lay down in his pile of newspapers. He thought about the whole journey and about how soon, this alley would no longer be his.

But the thought of Water staring into his eyes with such calm and caring was able to ease him into a comfortable sleep.

Destiny

Fire:
Volume V

Chapter 34

Hurricane walked back to the club at a very slow pace. His feet dragged across the ground, and his stomach rumbled with hunger. He knew that he would have to make up a story about why he was gone so long.

Three days. Better be a good story. Maybe I could say that I was taken prisoner by Snag's group. No, then they would confront Snag.

Hurricane puzzled with himself all the way to the alley. What would he say?

"Hurricane? Is that you?" Hurricane heard Link's voice.

No! Not yet!

"Uh, hi guys."

Link and Jax ran towards him and barreled him over. "Hurricane! Hurricane! Hurricane!" they shouted over and over. "You're back! You're really back!"

Hurricane stood up. He was surprised to get this kind of reaction from Link and Jax. "Can I please just get some food?"

They led him inside where everyone greeted him. "Hurricane!" "Is it really you?" "You're back!" "Hurricane's back!"

Hurricane spotted a yellow tabby among the crowd. She pushed everyone to the side in her urgency to get to him. "Hurricane! You're back! You're really back!"

Hurricane nodded and smiled. "Hi, Lexie."

Lexie rubbed her head against him. "I was so worried! I thought that I had lost my best friend!"

"I know. I thought I'd never be able to see anybody ever again."

"Where have you been all this time?"

Hurricane gulped. "Um, I was at, uh..."

"Hurricane!" Hurricane heard a voice behind him.

Saved by the bell.

Another yellow tabby walked up to Hurricane, followed closely by two guards.

"Hi, Fletch," Hurricane meowed.

"Hurricane, it's good to see you my friend. Everybody has been wondering where you've been."

"Yeah, okay," Hurricane replied, drowsily.

Lexie stepped between the two. "Hurricane needs to rest. Go be important somewhere else, Fletch."

Fletch pinned back his ears. "Fine, then. Hurricane, get some rest. Tomorrow, everyone will want to know why you've been gone for so long."

Hurricane nodded unenthusiastically. He trotted over to his sack and fell down with a thump. His bed felt like a billowy cloud compared to the dank, gloomy cell.

Lexie settled down beside him. "I'm not going to ask where you've been until tomorrow, no matter how much I'm dying to know. You need your rest. Deal?"

Hurricane was barely listening. "Sure." His eyes slowly started to close as a crowd of cats started circling his flour sack.

He sighed.

"Go away!" Lexie ordered. No one listened. Everybody wanted to know where the black-furred tom had been the past three days. They were all talking at once. Hurricane felt as though they were all news reporters that were hungry for a story. He could almost hear them saying things like "What's the scoop?" "What's the story, Hurricane?" "We're reporting to you live, straight from Hurricane's bed".

Lexie leaned to his ear. "They're like kittens bugging an old cat for a tale."

137

Hurricane groaned. "Or like a bunch of nosey news reporters crowding around for a story."

Lexie began threatening cats now. "I'm going to get Fletch's guards to take you away if you don't leave *right now*!" A few younger, more timid cats listened, and with a nod, scurried away. But the older cats were much more bold. They were intent on hearing a tale that would wow them.

"Go away!" Lexie kept shouting. But the crowd was louder.

"Where have you been, Hurricane?" one asked. "Why were you gone for so long?" questioned another.

Lexie was true to her word about Fletch's guards. "Fine, then. If they're not going to leave you alone, Hurricane, then I really will go get Fletch's Crowd Control Guards." Lexie left Hurricane to hide under his covers.

Go away, just go away!

Hurricane started glaring at the crowd. A few more skittered off at his angry look.

"Hurricane! Where were you?" A group of kittens pushed through the jumble of cats.

"Nowhere that concerns you idiots," Hurricane spat. The kittens crouched down, hurt.

"Oh, sorry," said a white one with orange patches. A larger black kitten with a white tail tip stepped up.

"Don't you talk to my friends like that, mister!" he hissed over the roaring of the crowd. They still wouldn't stop yapping!

"I'm ten times bigger than you, pipsqueak," Hurricane growled to the kitten. "Scat."

"I'm Fang Tip!" the kitten declared. "Because I can be tough if I want to be!"

"Fang Tip? Really? That's your name?" Hurricane rolled his eyes.

Fang Tip bristled the fur on his back. His tail whipped back and forth. "You'd better watch yourself, Fat Cat!" the kitten mocked.

"Oh, looks like the tough little kitty gave the even tougher kitty a nickname." Hurricane pushed away the towel and leaned in closer to the kitten. Part of the crowd got quiet, while another half got even louder. "Does the itty-bitty-tough-little-kitty want a nickname, too?"

Fang Tip flattened his ears.

"It's Scat Cat! You know why?"

Fang Tip hissed. "Why?" he spat.

"Because he needs to *scat!*" Hurricane swiped a sheathed paw at the kitten. He and his three companions scattered among the crowd. He didn't unsheathe his claws because that could get him kicked out of the Fletch Cat Club. Trying to hit a kitten with your claws unsheathed could be bad news, even though clawing a half-grown or full-grown cat didn't really mean much.

The crowd surged forward when Hurricane swiped. A cat leaped from it. "What's your problem?"

"My problem is that I can't get a decent nap with you freaks crowding me."

"You know that swiping at a kitten is against the rules, you idiot!"

"First of all, he looked like he could take care of himself." Hurricane lay on top of his towel on his sack. "Second of all, my claws were sheathed. Third of all, I didn't touch a whisker on the little guy. Not to mention, the rule is that you can't hit a kitten with your claws *unsheathed*. You also can't knock them to the ground when you hit them unless they're bullying another kitten. Did you see my claws? Did I knock him to the ground? Did I even touch him? No. So mind your own business, punk."

The cat whipped his tail from side to side. "Who are you calling a punk?"

Hurricane hopped off his bed and stood in front of the cat. He was yellowish with orange and red blotches. The red blaze on his face scrunched up as he tried to look tougher, but Hurricane could tell that the cat was a bit frightened by how the black tom was a bit taller. "You."

The cat began backing up. "Look, forget it. I'm sorry. Sleep, it's completely fine with me!"

Hurricane lowered his head. "What's your name, punk?"

"Skeeter. Skeeter, that's my name. Please, I'm sorry."

Hurricane was amused at this cat's fear. This must be how it felt to be a Dark Force. Fear is an accomplishment. It makes you feel overpowering. Hurricane nodded. "Got it. Now scat."

Skeeter turned tail and leapt back into the crowd. More shouting.

Shut up, shut up!

Suddenly, a small silver tabby kitten walked up. Her blue eyes twinkled with innocence.

Cute.

"Hello," she squeaked. "I'm Rainy. Are you Hurricane?"

"Um, yeah. Yeah, I am."

Rainy smiled up at him. He smiled back. "Are you the one that disappeared for three days?"

Hurricane sighed. "Yes. Are you one of Jasmine's kittens?"

Rainy shook her head, her tail sticking in the air. "No, I'm one of Angel's kittens. Jasmine's kittens are our friends though." Rainy tilted her head. "You know who Angel is, right?"

Hurricane nodded. "Of course I do. I know everyone here except for the kittens. Well, I know you and Fang Tip, now."

Rainy nodded. "I saw him get angry at you."

Hurricane leaned forward. "Yeah, well, he was just protecting his friends."

"He's thoughtful like that."

Hurricane laughed. "He seems a bit full of himself to me!"

140

Rainy squealed with laughter. "He just acts like that 'cause he's the oldest."

"Well, maybe you should tell him to lay off if he bosses you around all the time."

Rainy nodded enthusiastically. "Okay!" Her face went a bit serious again. "He just wants us to be safe, that's all."

Hurricane nudged her forward. "You get along back to Angel and your father, Stormy, now, okay?" Hurricane grinned. "Then you tell Ol' Scat Cat who's boss, got it?"

"Who?"

Hurricane gave a weak smile. "Fang Tip."

"Oh, okay. Got it!" Rainy skipped back off into the crowd. Hurricane winked at her as she glanced back.

Hurricane finally saw Lexie with three large tabbies at her side. One of them was Thorn from the other night with Stinger!

Lexie was speaking quickly to them. They nodded as she spoke and then scattered among the crowd.

"Move along, move along! It'll be the crate for ya'll if you don't!" A cat swarmed between bunches, chanting this the whole time. "Move along, move along!" The crate was almost like jail. If a cat did something really bad, then Fletch would determine how long they stayed in the crate. It was almost always less than a week. Fletch wasn't *that* strict.

Hurricane sighed with contentment as it started to work. The crowd began dispersing until it was down to a few stragglers who trotted up.

"Hurricane!" a young half-grown she-cat piped. "Where have you been?"

Hurricane groaned. "Can't you listen to the guards and 'move along, move along'?"

The she-cat's tail drooped. "But, can't you tell us?" She motioned to her two companions.

141

Hurricane sighed. Two other small, straggling groups of half-grown cats were waiting a few yards away. "Fine. Uh…"

He didn't know what to say!

"Well, I'll… announce it tomorrow! Fletch said that to me. That I would announce it tomorrow. Yes. I will announce why I was gone to everyone tomorrow." Hurricane flicked his tail. "So long."

The she-cat lowered her head. Her two companions, a tom and another she-cat, whispered something to each other. The tom stepped forward. His gray pelt was dappled with black spots.

"Hurricane? Please? We're in the middle of some training. We're becoming guards. We never even get to hear a story now and then! It's work, work, and work. No play! One story?"

Hurricane narrowed his eyes. "Then why did you decide to start training to be one, Bolt?"

Bolt rolled his eyes. "Because other cats look up to you, moron. Not to mention, I thought that it would be a good job for me. My trainer, Torch, said that I also have a lot of the right traits and strengths."

"Got'cha." Hurricane turned away from him.

Bolt gave up. He and the two she-cats walked away.

Hurricane turned back around and sighed. *Finally.* Lexie suddenly reappeared with a giant chip bag.

"Completely full! The things that humans throw away." Lexie tutted. She dropped it beside him. "Dig in."

Hurricane sunk his head into the bag. Lexie dragged him back out, chip crumbs all over his face.

"Do you have any idea how dangerous it is to do that?" Lexie shook her head. "No. I'll be right back."

Hurricane was left alone, staring at the bag.

Someone suddenly jumped at him from behind. He leapt up and swiped an unsheathed claw at whatever was on his back. It could be another Dark Force! But what he heard was a shrill shriek of surprise.

"Stop!" The cry came again.

A small silver shape jumped down in front of him.

It was Rainy.

Chapter 35

"Oh no," Hurricane said. He had swiped a claw at a kitten!

Rainy looked up at him in confusion. "Why did you try to hurt me?"

Hurricane shook his head. "No, I didn't know that it was you! I thought that you were… something else!"

Rainy stood there for a moment, unblinking. Then she smiled. "Okay."

Hurricane looked above her. Had anyone seen him?

"Are you going to tell me a story, now?" Rainy sat down with a sneeze.

She's even younger than Eco was!

Hurricane got off of his sack and sat down beside her. "A story about what?"

"About your disappearance."

Hurricane gulped. "Oh. Um…" Suddenly, Angel appeared.

"Where have you been, you little rascal?" Angel picked up her kitten by her scruff.

"But Mama!"

"No buts," Angel said through clenched teeth. Rainy started to whine very softly.

"Now I don't want any of that tonight, Rainy." Angel rolled her eyes. "Kittens!" she said to Hurricane with a groan. "You can never get them to listen, can you?"

Hurricane laughed and touched his nose to Rainy's. "Goodnight. Sleep tight."

Rainy stopped wailing. "Okay. Goodnight. Will you play with me tomorrow?"

"Hurricane's going to be very busy tomorrow, Rainy," Angel pointed out to her kitten.

"But-"

"We're going back to our bed. Your siblings want to see you."

Angel walked away with a very upset kitten.

Lexie reappeared with a napkin. "Here." Lexie set the napkin down and clawed a few chips onto it. "Now you can eat."

Hurricane ate the chips with pleasure. "Mmm."

Lexie smiled. "Get some rest. You'll be up on the top shelf telling Fletch about your journey tomorrow." With the flick of an ear, she turned and left.

Hurricane clawed out more chips. The crunching noise started to make him sleepy. A huge yawn came out of him. He stretched and closed his eyes.

Beautiful images met his mind. A field of waving green as far as the eye could see, dotted with flowers of every color. The bright golden sun sent rays of light down to the grass and made it shine with beauty. The forest was to his right. But to his left nothing hindered his view of the baby blue sky. It took him a moment to realize that he was simply dreaming.

Too bad. I would love to be in this place forever.

"Yes, sorrowful, isn't it? To realize that it is nothing more than a dream."

Hurricane didn't turn around. He knew to whom the voice belonged. It belonged to the definition of evil.

The Dark Lord was after him again.

"Go away, Than," Hurricane ordered without turning.

"Ah, using names now, are we? Are titles too old fashioned?"

"Stay out of my dreams."

"Am I intruding, Hurricane? Don't you want to chat?"

Hurricane spun around and leaped at the Dark Lord, claws outstretched. "Go away!"

The Lord of Eternal Darkness disappeared from in front of the black, blue-eyed tom. He heard a voice behind himself.

"You're dreaming, Hurricane. Even if you could catch me before I disappear, which I doubt you can, you wouldn't in any way injure me. Much less kill me."

Hurricane turned around and faced the huge reptile. "Fine. If I can't fight you here, then I'll find somewhere else."

"We could fight now, if you like, kitty-cat. I know a place."

"No. Not now. It's not the right time."

"Alright," the Dark Lord said, pretending to be offended. "You win. But we'll meet again soon Hurricane. I guarantee it." With the snap of his menacingly sharp claws, he was gone.

Hurricane stepped backwards and stood there for a moment. He wasn't completely sure that the Lord of Darkness was gone yet. After a few seconds, he decided he was safe. A butterfly flew past his head, and he felt like a carefree kitten again. He chased after the colorful creature all the way to the trees. The little speck of yellow blue and green disappeared into the canopies.

Hurricane stared up for a moment. Why did he feel so insecure? He took a step back, still staring at where the colorful insect had disappeared. The leaves suddenly rustled and the butterfly fluttered over to a nearby flower.

Hurricane stepped in front of the fragile creature and kept staring into the treetop. More rustling. "Hello?" He asked into the green, slightly pulling back his head. The rustling suddenly stopped. It was quiet.

Too quiet.

Hurricane gave the leaves one last glare and relaxed. Just then, a huge snake the size of a car came hurtling down on top of him, its menacing fangs glinting cruelly. Hurricane screeched and was submerged in a mixture of darkness and pain.

Hurricane woke with a gasp. He coughed and coughed, working hard to recapture his breath. A stinging sensation was burning in his chest. When he looked down, two teeth marks were bleeding nonstop.

"It actually bit me!" He whispered to himself.

"*Don't worry, Hurricane. Wounds from dreams won't hurt you. But if that Dark Force snake had bitten you in an awake state, you would already be dead.*" A deep satisfied laugh echoed around Hurricane until it faded to nothing more than a whisper.

Hurricane shivered as the voice faded into a hissing silence, and bent his head to lick the bleeding fang marks. They were soon hidden beneath the black sea of his fur.

Hurricane raised his head determinedly. "You can't have me, Than. I'm not your prisoner anymore."

Chapter 36

Hurricane stretched the next morning and began to quietly step over to the entrance. He glanced around. He didn't want to be peppered with endless questions like yesterday.

"Hurricane?" a small voice peeped. "Where are you going?" Hurricane silently turned his head towards the voice. The same young, silver-tabby, blue-eyed kitten stood before him.

"Rainy, I'm going hunting right now."

"Will you please play with me?" Rainy tucked her tail between her legs and lowered her head to make herself look cute. "My daddy is always busy 'cause he's a guard. My mama is never able to play because my siblings are always getting into trouble."

Hurricane sighed. He wanted to get out of here before other cats started waking up. "Rainy, please..."

Rainy looked at him with sad eyes.

Hurricane rolled his eyes. Rainy wasn't giving up. He looked towards where Angel usually slept. She was still softly snoring. Hurricane looked back at Rainy. Perhaps he could take her out for a little while? If he got her back to the club before Angel woke up, she would never have to find out.

Hurricane completely turned his body towards Rainy. "Okay. But you need to stay at my side at all times, understand?"

Rainy's eyes brightened. "Okay!"

"If I lose sight of you for a split-second even, it's back to the club-fort, got it?"

Rainy nodded enthusiastically. "Yeah!"

"Then come on." Hurricane headed towards the entrance, the little kitten hard on his heels.

When Hurricane got to the entrance, the two Entrance Guards halted him. It wasn't Jax and Link this time. One was a black and white tom with splashes of orange, while the other was just a solid tan.

"Hello, sirs. May I pass?"

"Looks like your little adventure knocked some respect for superiority into you, didn't it, Hurricane?" the tan one sneered. The colorful one shot him a cautious glance, but said nothing.

"What are you talking about?"

"Link and Jax are always complaining about how you never have any respect for authority. True?"

Hurricane groaned and picked up Rainy in his mouth. The two Entrance Guards didn't protest as he walked out with the delicate kitten. Hurricane set Rainy down on the other side of the entrance. The alley outside was dark and cold. Rainy shivered. "Is it always this cold?"

Hurricane fluffed out his fur to get warm and pulled Rainy closer. "It's nearly winter. Winters are chilly in New York."

Rainy pinned back her ears and copied Hurricane's actions of fluffing out his fur. Her tiny silver tail stuck straight up. "So where are we going first?" Her body gave signs that she was chilled already, but her bright blue eyes reflected excitement. "I want to catch a bird!"

Hurricane looked above them. Perched on the power line that strung from the pottery shop to the restaurant was a small gray pigeon. The little bird sat with its feathers fluffed out like Hurricane's fur. Hurricane laughed quietly to himself.

"What's so funny?" Rainy asked immediately.

Hurricane straightened his neck. "Funny? Oh, nothing. I was just thinking about what you said."

"You'll help me catch a bird, right?"

Hurricane smiled. "Maybe we should start with some easier prey items. For instance, perhaps, ground animals? Like mice?"

Rainy thought for a moment before she replied. "Okay."

Hurricane led the tabby out of the chilly narrow alleyway. Her fur was buffeted by a blast of wind that carried the chill. She let out a small squeak of surprise. Hurricane nudged her forward with his nose. "Keep going."

Hurricane was beginning to think that this was a bad idea. Why had he ever even considered bringing a kitten outside? Perhaps he should turn back.

Rainy let out a little squeal of delight as something caught her eye. Hurricane swung his head in the direction she was facing. A small mouse was scuttling across the sidewalk. It was heading towards a crack in a building. Hurricane crouched down. "Watch closely."

Rainy nodded and stepped aside. Hurricane's tail whipped back and forth as he bunched his legs. Hurricane launched himself forward, bearing down on the puny creature. The mouse squeaked in fear and scurried towards the crack as fast as his little legs would carry him. Hurricane swiped at the mouse with his right paw, catching its tail in his claws.

"Stop! Stop, please!"

Hurricane yowled in surprise and threw the mouse back to the ground.

The mouse had just talked to him!

Rainy let out a shrill whine and hid behind Hurricane's night-black build.

The mouse leaned against the building. "Thank goodness!" it gasped. "I truly thought I was done for! Fantastic hunting skills cat, bravo."

Hurricane was amazingly confused. Not only had this mouse just spoken to him, now it was congratulating him on his effort to hunt him down!

"You... talk?"

The mouse stood on *two legs* and dusted himself off. "Well, yes, of course. Anyone who was sent by the Sighters *must* be able to talk, am I correct?"

Hurricane straightened his ears. "Excuse me?" Had the Sighters decided to send them for the fourth element already?

The mouse bowed formally and smiled. "My name is Marvin. Marvin Mouse, to be precise. What might your name be, kind gentlemen? I suspect Hurricane is the correct answer, or I'm afraid I'm in the wrong place, yes?"

Hurricane nodded slowly. "Yeah. I'm Hurricane."

"Your companion, or perhaps *partner*, is Shade, is he not?"

"Yes, he is."

Rainy bounded out from behind Hurricane's sitting form. "Aren't we supposed to be hunting him?"

"Ack!" cried Marvin at Rainy's remark.

"No, Rainy. Not this mouse. He's... special, I guess." Hurricane pinned back his ears in discomfort. He didn't like the fact that this *Marvin* was being sent to find him already. He'd been home for only one night!

Marvin waved a paw at Rainy vigorously. His tiny black button-eyes were wild with fear. "Back away, cat! I'm not tasty! Trust me on that! I'm a slimy muck, I am! Certainly, *this* muscle is not something you would enjoy devouring!"

Hurricane had to hold back a laugh. Even when this tiny rodent thought he was about to get shredded by a feline, he still refused to use improper grammar. "Excuse my little friend here," Hurricane apologized. He stretched out a paw towards Rainy to pull her between his two front legs. "This pesky kitten is Rainy, if you're wondering."

Rainy struck out a sheathed paw and swiped the empty air, giggling while doing so. "Hurricane is my friend! He's teaching me how to hunt." Rainy turned towards Hurricane and put her front paws on his chest. "I'm his favorite kitten!" she mewed, smiling a mile wide.

Hurricane flicked an ear and lifted his brow. "Now Rainy, choosing favorites can lead to disagreements. Your friends might get mad at you."

"But aren't I?" Rainy seemed to have forgotten that Marvin was standing there.

Hurricane leaned over and quickly rubbed his cheek against Rainy's. "You're a good little cat, Rainy, I'll tell you that."

"I hate to break up such a heart-warming conversation, but have you both forgotten that there is a *talking mouse* standing before you?"

Hurricane let a small uneasy laugh slip. Rainy took her paws off his chest and sat down in-between his legs, turning her tiny silver body toward Marvin. "Sorry, Marvin. So, will you tell us why-"

"What are Sighters, Hurricane?" Rainy impatiently broke in.

Hurricane groaned. She needed to let him talk! "Rainy, please be quiet for a minute."

"What are they? What are See-ers? I want to know! Tell me, please? Please!"

"*Sighters.* Not See-ers. Rainy, just calm down and be quiet. I need to talk to this... this *Marvin* fellow."

"But-"

"*No.*" Hurricane said firmly. Rainy shrank deeper between his legs. He strengthened his forearms around the tiny kitten and leaned forward a bit, making sure that she didn't scurry away out of fear. Hurricane turned his gaze to Marvin once more. "Now, tell me. Why did the Sighters send you?" Hurricane was relieved that his tiny silver bundle hadn't interrupted. He caught a glimpse of her ice-blue eyes brightening at the chance to finally see why the talking rodent was there.

Marvin gave a quick "ahem" before speaking, and that was the first time that Hurricane noticed a small red scarf around his neck. "The Sighters have sent me to inform you that, in three days time, you will be sent to search for the fourth and final element."

Rainy couldn't bear it any longer. "Fourth element? Sighters? Talking mice? Oh Hurricane, tell me!"

Hurricane ignored Rainy and stared into the depths of Marvin's eyes. Three days? Were the Sighters *trying* to exhaust him? "Why so soon?"

Marvin gave a nervous twitch of his whiskers. His troubled gaze fell on Rainy, and then drifted back to Hurricane without a word. Hurricane nodded, understanding filling his blue irises. "Rainy, could you head back to the club for a bit?"

"But we were going to hunt!"

Hurricane gave her a demanding glare, and with an annoyed moan, she hopped out of Hurricane's forearm trap and scuttled back around the corner to the alley.

The faces of the tan tom and the black-and-white tom with silver flecks flashed through his mind. "Don't tell Spur and Buck about Marvin!" he called after her.

He heard a grunt from Rainy, and her stubby tabby tail disappeared around the corner.

"Okay. So, why exactly are you here?" Hurricane was curious about Marvin. He knew that there were cat and dog Sighters, but mice were unheard of.

"I'm a simple messenger, Hurricane. There is simply not much more to it." Marvin quickly passed his paws over his whiskers and kept speaking. "The world of Sighters is filled with magical phenomena, including talking mice such as myself." Marvin hopped on top of a slab of concrete that had come out of the sidewalk to make himself appear taller. "I am not one of the Sighter community, but I do live within their world, watching and listening. Mice are constantly given jobs as messengers by Sighters, and it is a great honor."

Hurricane's tail tip rippled slowly as he thought. Did this mouse have more to tell him?

"Why do they want me to come and find the next element so soon? Do they *want* me to pass out?" The steady rippling of his tail turned into an annoyed lashing.

Marvin flattened back his ears. Hurricane could tell that Marvin was uncomfortable to be so close to an angry cat. "The Dark Forces have been greatly angered by your escape. The Sighters feel that this will lead to a much earlier attack than we had expected. A group of Sighters were listening to the whispering news and warnings of rock, river, soil and sky. The air around them was echoing a threat, and they quickly detected the Dark Lord's anger on the breeze. They've become cautious, and they believe that the last element should be collected as soon as possible."

Hurricane now felt less resentful about this, and urgency overwhelmed him. If they didn't find the next element soon, darkness would blanket the Earth and the Dark Lord would rule all he saw. The shadows would expand, and the horrors within them would creep out, relishing in the openness and destroying whatever they pleased.

"Thank you, Marvin. That's helpful to know."

Marvin dipped his head. "My pleasure, cat. Now, off to find your partner, Shade, is it? Yes, that's it. Well, good day to you!" With that, Marvin leapt off of his perch on the concrete slab and slipped through a crack in the building to Hurricane's right. Hurricane stood there until he could no longer hear the scurrying and scratching of Marvin's tiny paws. Once there was no more trace of him but a stale scent on the breeze, Hurricane turned and galloped around the corner, where he saw Buck and Spur guarding the entrance outside.

Spur turned his tortoiseshell head to Hurricane and smiled. But Buck simply looked at him with a displeased frown. His tan pelt was ruffled against the cold.

"Hello, Spur." Hurricane nodded to the black-and-white-orange-speckled tom. "Buck," Hurricane simply said in a reluctant greeting. Buck had always been an annoying grouch. All three of them were the same age, but Buck always acted as though he were older and more superior. Spur and Hurricane were never exactly close friends, but Spur wasn't ever mean to anyone, quite the contrary. He was kind and calm, and always seemed a bit submissive. Hurricane was surprised that the Guard Training Class had even accepted such a shy cat.

Buck grunted. "You let a kitten that was in no way closely related to you come outside. I thought she was your sister or something until I recognized her." Buck spat on the ground. Both Hurricane and Spur made a face, but Buck ignored them. "I might have to report this to Fletch, you inconsiderate scrap."

Spur's eyes widened, but he continued to say nothing. Hurricane pinned back his ears. "Who are you calling an inconsiderate scrap?"

Buck lifted his head higher, smirking.

Hurricane let a snarl slip. "First of all, I was originally going hunting. She wouldn't stop bugging me until I let her come, so I did. She came back in one piece, didn't she? Isn't that all that matters?"

"Not according to my Guard Training, it doesn't." Buck passed his tongue across his muzzle.

Hurricane hissed. "You think that you're so much better than the rest of us because you passed your stupid training with flying colors.

154

Well, whoop-dee-doo for you." Hurricane paused. "That doesn't give you an excuse to treat the rest of us like trash!"

Buck seemed too stunned to speak for a moment. No one had ever talked to him like that before. But he quickly retaliated. "Hey, you're the one that decided not to train for it."

Hurricane narrowed his eyes. He had decided not to train to be a Guard when he was a young cat because he was afraid. He had seen the Guards in Training, and they looked in pain and exhausted. He hadn't understood why they wanted to train for it. At least, it wasn't until afterwards that he did. All the guards were treated like kings, and kittens and young Guards in Training always crowded retired Guards for stories about their days in the spotlight. Hurricane had even listened to a few of those stories as a young cat, when he had actually had time to do so.

"I know I made a bad choice, but the past is the past. I would have liked to become a Guard, but that opportunity is gone now. So don't nag at me about it, *capisci*?"

Buck snorted. "Whatever you say, Tornado."

"*Hurricane*," he spat.

"Hurricane, Tornado, they're all the same concept, storms that swirl around. Except that one is bigger and goes over water."

Hurricane's fur bristled, and he lowered his head to make it level with his body as he padded inside. The sky was turning purple, signaling that the sun was about to rise.

"May as well call you Shadow, since that's your proper name," Buck remarked.

Hurricane kept walking. Buck could call him what he pleased. It didn't make any difference. If everyone else called him Hurricane, that was fine by him.

His eyes caught Rainy, chattering away to her three brothers and her sister. Angel was till sleepy, but she listened to Rainy's ranting.

"Then Marvin yelled 'ack!' It was really funny! Then he started shouting all these silly reasons for me not to eat him!"

Hurricane's blood went cold. She was telling her family about Marvin and the Sighters!

155

Chapter 37

Hurricane wasn't sure whether to race over and quiet her or pretend that he wasn't there. Then another thought struck him and twisted a knot in his stomach. Now Angel knew that he had taken Rainy outside! Hurricane had to think fast. He turned left and stayed against the wall, crouching low.

A young golden colored cat at the edge of the crowd looked at him, puzzled. "Hurricane? What are you doing?"

Hurricane felt his muscles tense in frustration. He got that cold, shivering, tense feeling that you get in your stomach, chest and spine when you realize that your homework isn't in your backpack, or when you hear a creaking sound downstairs at night. Hurricane *hated* that feeling. He simply shot a glance at the cat and said, "practicing my hunting skills. Now get back to your studying, Leo!" Hurricane shot away from Leo and disappeared among the crowd.

A few cats got up and began pestering him with questions about his disappearance. But Hurricane quickly silenced them and sat them back down with an angry hiss. He proceeded on through the crowd, hissing and crouching, until he got to Lexie's bed. "Lexie!" He pleaded. "Get up!"

The yellow tabby groaned and rolled over, fluffing out her fur. Hurricane gave her a shake with his front paws. "Ungh... What...?"

Hurricane shook harder. "Wake up! Help me! I need to hide!"

Lexie's eyes shot open. "Hide? From what? Is it Snag?" Lexie was on her paws now.

"No. I took Angel's kitten, Rainy, outside. Now she's telling Angel all about it."

Lexie stared at him. "You took her *outside*? Hurricane, why would you do that?"

"Because she wouldn't stop bugging me until I did!"

"Hurricane! You know that's against the rules!" Lexie didn't seem angry, more worried.

"I know!" he hissed. "Just hide me!"

156

"Hurricane, we live in a storage room. She'll find you faster than you can say 'mouse'."

"*I know*! It's just for a bit. Please!"

Lexie sighed defeat. "Fine. You knew I would say yes at some point." There was a hint of amusement in her voice.

Hurricane crouched down beside her. But it was only a few seconds before he swung his head around to find Angel's mate, Stormy, towering over him. He felt Lexie tense beside him.

"We have a lot to discuss," Stormy growled.

Chapter 38

Shade lay curled up once more in his bed of newspapers. He longed for sleep to come, but it never did. He sat worrying over the element of Fire, and the fact that the Dark Lord was becoming more and more bold. Soon he would be right there in New York, crashing and burning all he saw.

Shade sighed. He rolled over onto his back and shifted the elements of Earth and Water in-between his paws. Doing this made him feel a bit better. Shade studied the embroidered letters on the two pouches. He wondered how a dog could stitch that with its paws. Then he remembered that Sighters could use magic.

But if Sighters could use magic, then why didn't Everest use magic on their journey for the Water element?

Shade had just begun to puzzle over this when Snag appeared.

"Well, Shady-boy? What's your decision? Are you going to join us or not?"

The question took Shade by surprise. "You said that I have three days. You've only given me two. I'll give you my decision tomorrow."

Snag creased his brow. "Fine. Tomorrow it is, then."

Just as they were turning to leave, Shade noticed a new dog tagging along in the gang. She was a small, brown and gray mutt with one pointed ear, and one ear that stuck up then flopped over halfway. Something about her looked strangely familiar. He recognized the shape and face of this dog from somewhere.

Eclipse?

No, this wasn't Shade's captured parent. If it were his mother, he would have immediately recognized her. But this dog resembled so many of his mother's traits that it baffled him to even consider that it wasn't her at all. He knew this dog, though he never met her. Was it his mother's sibling? It couldn't be; this dog looked about the age of Shade. Even her scent was familiar, which was the main thing that Shade was confused by.

"Excuse me?" Shade quietly asked her as the rest of Snag's group began running ahead. The she-dog seemed uneasy around Shade.

"Please, I need to catch up with my group. Snag will have my tail if I fall behind." The dog started to speed up.

"Wait. Do I know you from somewhere?" Shade wouldn't give up until he knew this dog's name.

The dog was beginning to get a frustrated look on her face. "No. I've never met you in my life. Now leave me alone!" The dog gave a quick growl deep in her throat, then spun around and raced after the departing group. Shade heard a few sharp words from Snag for her falling behind, then they all turned the corner and left.

Shade sat down, blinking in frustration. Who was that dog? Her pelt, the face, her walking gait, so much like his mother. Even the scent seemed oddly familiar. He had to know her. He knew that if he thought hard enough, he'd recall where it was that they had met before. Why he recognized her. Who she was.

Then it hit him. He'd never met this dog in his lifetime, but he knew her.

That dog was his sister!

Chapter 39

Shade followed the gradually fading scent trail down the road. Snag and his group had a camp or settlement somewhere, he was sure of it. He knew this because they came from the same direction every morning, and went back in the same direction every evening. Sometimes at night, though, because they hang out at midnight now and then.

Shade finally came to a much more rundown place in the city. There were ratty shacks and tenements randomly set on either side of a cracked road, and a few flickering streetlamps were lined along it. Trash was strewn though the yards, while graffiti covered the surrounding walls and cement. A few street signs even had drawings on them.

Yikes.

Shade trotted through the ugly housing and shot around the corner. The scent led him to an alley covered in graffiti and litter. A few trashcans looked as though they had been tipped over by hungry strays that had been desperate for a decent meal. A shopping cart full of cans and boxes stood creaking by the wall. Shade almost tripped over it in his rush to get out. Finally, the opening came into view.

Once Shade emerged from the trashed alleyway, he stopped to see a tall, light brown picket fence before him. To his left and right were some narrow roads, about the size of an alley. At the end of the road to his left stood trees and bushes, while the one to his right led to more shacks. But the scent didn't lead to his left or his right. It led straight ahead, through the fence. When he looked closer, Shade noticed a hole at the bottom of the fence, just big enough for a dog to squeeze through. He noticed multiple colors of fur clinging the wood around the hole. Shade realized that it was the entrance to Snag's camp. He pressed his furry self through the hole. In his attempt to push through, his blue bandanna was caught on a piece of splintered wood. *Never mind that.* When he got inside, he froze.

Shade had just set paw in a junkyard. Old cars, sofas, cans, boxes, anything that you could think of to throw away was here. The scent was strongest in this place. A path had been made between the piles of trash for someone to walk through without having to clamber over piles upon piles of junk. Shade still had to swerve around pieces of shattered glass and metal, though.

The scent became stronger and stronger as he wove deeper into the junkyard. Finally, he rounded a pile of old tires and was scared out of his fur to see two Doberman-looking dogs guarding the entrance to a clearing. In the center of the dirt clearing was a pile of wooden planks and cars. A few boxes were scattered over the pile. Dogs were all around the area, racing, fighting, eating, sleeping. A few dogs were coming in and out of an opening in the junk pile. Shade wanted to race in and see what was inside, but the Doberman mutts were blocking the entrance. Shade began to rethink his idea. Maybe he should just leave.

That's when he saw his sister. She looked hungry and tired. Definitely not happy, that was for sure. Beside her was the pup that he had seen at Deacon's a few days earlier. His sister seemed to be having a conversation with the pup.

"It's okay, Snag can't be bad for ever. He'll give in to us when he sees our pain."

"But when?" the pup protested.

"I don't know. Now get back to your mother and father. I have work to do."

"Okay," the pup grunted as he turned to walk away. "Bye."

Shade's sister smiled weakly, then walked on. She turned and started walking toward the entrance, right in Shade's direction!

Shade's sister walked up to the dogs on guard. "May I leave for a bit?"

"To go where?" one of the dogs growled.

"For a walk."

The Doberman mutts thought for a moment, then nodded. "Be back in thirty minutes."

She nodded, rolling her eyes. As she walked out, Shade shrank back, out of sight. Should he really go through with this? Yes, he must.

He silently followed her as she confidently picked her way through the piles of garbage. Finally, she crawled through the hole in the fence and disappeared. Shade followed.

Once they were outside, Shade trotted after her as she slipped through the alley with the shopping cart. Shade held back a few feet to keep her from noticing him. They emerged from the alley into the

161

sunlight. The moment they were out, the dog spun around and leapt at Shade. "Stop following me!"

Shade was surprised. How did she know he was there? "Get off of me!"

His sister stepped back and let him get up. "Why are you following me? What do you want?"

Shade sighed. He wondered how she would react when he told her. "You need to know something. Something important."

His sister pinned back her ears. "Tell me who you are, first."

Shade straightened his neck. "My name's Shade. I'm your brother."

Chapter 40

"You're my *what?*" Shade's sister looked as though she would fall off of her own paws at any moment.

"Your brother. Look." Shade pressed his paw into a pile of dirt. "Now you."

Shade's sister looked confused, but did as he said. She pressed her own paw next to his. The prints were identical. "That doesn't prove anything," she insisted. "We're both dogs. Of course our prints are the same." She began to back up in an attempt to run.

Shade had to make her understand. She couldn't leave. "Don't be an idiot. I mean, look at our fur. The blacks and grays are the same shades."

Shade's sister looked reluctant still. "You're not my brother! I've never known you in my life!"

"Neither have I." Shade tried to keep his voice level. "But I can tell. Our scents are alike."

"So?" She growled.

"My mother was named Eclipse."

Shade's sister went silent, her eyes wide as moons. "Eclipse?"

"Yes."

Shade's sister stepped back, shaking her head. "*Eclipse?* How?"

Shade didn't answer.

His sister looked up. "My name's Bailey."

Shade nodded. "Bailey. I like it."

Bailey still looked shocked. "But I never knew you as a pup. How are we siblings?"

Shade thought for a moment. "Maybe we just share a mother. My father was a wolf named Rebel."

"My father was a mutt named Baird."

"That's it. We're half-siblings."

"I was born at a puppy-mill," Bailey stated.

Shade's blood went cold. His mother was stuck in a *puppy-mill?* "A puppy-mill?"

"Yeah, I know."

Shade shook his head at Bailey. "Is she okay?"

"I don't know," Bailey answered. "I left pretty early. I got to some person's house and the second they opened the door I saw my chance. I've been on my own ever since."

Shade nodded.

"I saw where you live. That alley seems really lonely. Life must be pretty boring, huh?"

Shade nodded hesitantly, laughing on the inside. If only she knew.

"What's with the collar?" Bailey asked coolly. "E.W.? That a name some human gave you?" Shade lowered his gaze. Should he just make something up?

"Well, uh, it's kind of a long story, I guess, but..."

"I have time," Bailey answered.

Shade turned his head away, thinking. Then he made his decision.

"Come with me." Shade stepped backwards a few feet, and motioned for her to follow him with his head.

"Why? Can't you just tell me here?"

"No."

"Oh. Um, okay."

Bailey padded after Shade. The wolf-dog led his sister around a corner. He decided to take the right; it looked as though too many humans would live around there for many dogs' likings. That meant that fewer strays would be able to overhear Shade's shocking news.

Shade turned back to Bailey once he was sure that they were out of earshot of any dogs that might be lingering around Snag's camp. He sniffed the air, just to be sure. There were so many dog scents that it was hard to tell, but from what he could smell, no one was nearby.

"Okay, when I tell you this, don't freak out, got it?"

Bailey pinned back her ears. "It must be bad if you're worried about me getting upset."

Shade rolled his eyes. "Whatever. Just listen."

Bailey nodded, showing small signs of uncertainty.

"Okay," Shade began. He was still wondering if this was a bad idea. But Bailey was his sister. He could trust her, right? "This is why I have this 'collar'. You see, it's not a collar. They're pouches, given to me by wolves and cats that you'll never even believe."

"What? Can they fly or something?" Bailey smiled, holding in a laugh.

Shade bit back a retort. He recalled Air, her long, graceful, feathery white wings that enabled her to soar like an eagle. "Well..."

Bailey raised her brow. "'*Well*?' I ask you if they can fly and you say '*well*?'"

"Just let me finish."

Bailey shook her head. "Fine. Go on."

"Look. These pouches hold items more powerful than anything on Earth. In fact, only I and one other can hold these things without total destruction happening. Got it?"

Bailey's playful expression disappeared, only to be replaced by a look of unease. "Shade..."

"Don't worry," Shade reassured his slightly younger sister. "I won't let it hurt you. Just listen, okay?"

165

Bailey nodded, her face serious now.

Shade started speaking fast, using a lot of slang. "Here's how it all started: it was raining, see? So I decided to find a place that actually had a roof. I get out of my alley, I run into Snag, right? Well, I'm all grumpy that day, so I have the brilliant idea of back-talking Snag and his group. They try to get me for it, so I run down the street, fast as lightning. Well, I barrel into this cat, who says that he knows where shelter is. I follow him, which makes him angry. But I keep following him anyway. So at one point, we get into a conversation, and I found out that his name is Shadow, but he calls himself Hurricane. I tell him that I'm Shade. So we get to this rundown house and go inside. I shout, 'hello?' after Hurricane's gone upstairs to check the place out. Well, I hear this voice, see? It goes, 'No, only me, Shade'. Well I'm scared out of my fur, so I whip around to see this really beat up dog with an eye-patch. The guy's got more scars than anybody I've seen in my life. But the dude's got muscle, I'll tell you that much. He's kind of a tan color, with pointy ears; one has a claw tear through it. Course, now it has two, 'cause I had to fight him once and I made another mark, but I'll tell you that in a sec'. Anyway, the dog calls himself Everest, and that's where it all started." Shade began spilling everything out. The Sighters, the Elements, element keepers, the guides, the Dark Lord, the Dark Forces, Banshee the raven, everything. He also told her about Air and the fight with Banshee, which made Bailey apologize for being rude about them flying.

Once Shade had finished, Bailey was speechless. The look on her face expressed amazement and horror. "Eternal darkness?"

"Yeah."

"Oh my God." Bailey let out a whine of distress. "Shade, what are we going to do?"

"You're going to swear not to tell anyone about this, that's what you're going to do." Bailey lowered her head. "I'm going to do my job and finish this. The world depends on Hurricane and me, so we have the responsibility of saving it. Lucky us."

Bailey cocked her head. "Why can't one of those... those Sight-y-ers do it?"

Shade frowned. "Sighters. I don't know. Hurricane and I were 'chosen'."

"So?" Bailey growled. Shade shook his head.

"It's hard to explain. Look, you've *got* to keep this a secret, okay? You need to swear that you won't tell anyone, got it?"

Bailey groaned. "How can I keep that a secret? I have to tell the York Pack!"

Shade narrowed his eyes. "So that's what Snag calls it, huh?"

Bailey's tail drooped. "I was forced to join, okay?

Shade showed his teeth. "Snag's a jerk! Why would you join *his* stupid super-pack? You know that he bullies me all the time with his original little gang that he had before the 'York Pack', right?"

Bailey's eyes widened. "Oh, I only saw him speak to you that one time, a few hours ago."

Shade grunted in reply. "Anyway, how did you wind up in his pack in the first place?"

Bailey dragged her gaze away from Shade. "Well, I used to live in this shed. Alone. Snag found me, passing on his news about the York Pack. I refused at first. I didn't really want to have to listen to an alpha. He said he'd give me time and come back another day. So two days pass. I go about my life as usual until he shows up again. This time, he doesn't force it on me. Instead, he starts telling me all the benefits of being in a pack. Strength in numbers, more dogs to catch food, shelter, you know? It sounded kind of nice, so I told him I'd think about it. He said that he'd come back the next day. He did. He was a bit firmer this time, so I said maybe. He said that I'd had a whole night to think about it, and that it was a yes or no question. He leans in real close and gives me this burning look when he says yes or *no*. So, of course, I give in immediately and say yes. He tells me that I made the right choice, and to follow him. I go with his little group to the junkyard, where a bunch of other dogs were. When Snag walked in, everyone howled. That's how they greet him, since he's their leader. When he walks by, they nod at him all formally. It's stupid. Not to mention, he and his guards treat all of us like trash. They have us all jailed up in that place."

Shade sighed. "So they won't let you out?"

Bailey shook her head.

"Why?"

Bailey bared her teeth. "Because he wants us to be his servants. That Snag will do anything to get what he wants! His stupid guards are no better. He gives them the special treatment, so they make the rest of us be their servants, too! He even threatened to beat a pup yesterday when the little guy asked to resign. He didn't want to be a pack member anymore, and Snag wouldn't stand for it. He said that if the pup didn't reconsider, he'd be beaten senseless. So, of course, he stayed."

Shade winced when his half-sister said, "beaten". "Why don't you just ask to go for a walk and not come back?"

Bailey sighed. "They'll hunt you down, no questions asked. Those dogs are related to bloodhounds I tell you. Then when they do, you'll wish you were never born. Trust me, the punishment isn't pretty."

"Just cross the state border. It'd be a cinch."

"You make it sound so easy." Bailey sat down. "You and I both know that that's harder than it sounds. Getting across the border would take forever. Garbage cans aren't behind every tree, you know that. I'm not a very good hunter, so I'd probably starve at some point." Bailey took a moment to lick her paw. "I'm more of a dumpster-diver, not a hunter."

Shade cocked his head. "I could teach you. I'm pretty good at it. I get it from my dad, I think."

"Shade, enough with the stupid 'crossing-the-border' fantasy! This is real."

Shade coughed. "Sorry."

"Whatever. Look, I need to get back. This is a lot to take in, and I need time to think it over. Go away. It's not safe, definitely not alone. Get out of here, fast as you can. They've probably already caught your scent back at the junkyard."

Shade gulped. He hadn't even given a thought to disguising his scent when he got in. "Okay. Bye Bailey, I'll see you again soon, I hope."

Bailey nodded. "I'll try to be on the next Pick-Up Patrol."

"What?"

"That's the little group of dogs Snag drags around when he's out to pick up new members. He calls it a Pick-Up Patrol. The patrol is usually made up of the dogs that were in his original little gang. But sometimes, he takes new members around, too."

"Oh. Okay." Shade stepped backwards a bit. "Well, I might see you tomorrow. That's when Snag says he's going to come pick me up."

Bailey flattened her ears. "Leave. Leave the city."

"Wait, what? Why?"

"The York Pack is a nightmare. You don't want to be part of it Shade, you just don't."

Shade lowered his head. "I'm not running away. I'm needed here. I have to save us. Hurricane and I, we've got to stay."

"Shade, please-"

Shade cut her off. "Bailey, no. I'm not leaving. I'm not a coward; I'll stand my ground. And I have to save the world. I have a destiny, Bailey. I have a destiny."

Chapter 41

Icy claws of cold speared through Shade's skin as he padded silently back. Once he had turned onto his street, he let out a sigh of relief. Home at last.

Shade pictured curling comfortably into his bed of newspapers. He would fall asleep calmly, and relish the feeling of rest. He couldn't wait. But when he turned into his alley, not only did a warm bed meet him, but a mouse as well.

"Oh dear, where is that dog?" the mouse fretted, still not noticing Shade. "They said that he would be here, but are they correct? Of course not! Their old foggy minds are always giving the wrong information. They *say* they can tell the future, but *no*. He's. Not. Here."

A talking mouse? A talking mouse! What the…

Shade lifted a paw. "Excuse me, but, uh, are you looking for someone?"

The mouse whipped around and let out a squeak of shock. "Dog!" The mouse slipped under Shade's bed and disappeared.

Shade cocked his head. "Um, hello? Do you need something? Because if not, then you can leave." Shade was used to overly strange things by now, so a talking mouse barely fazed him.

The mouse peeked out from under the papers. "State your name, fiend!"

Shade peeled back his lips in a snarl. "'*Fiend*'?"

The mouse jerked his head backwards. "I mean, 'sir'."

"Better," Shade growled. "My name's Shade, if you got to know."

The mouse perked up immediately after Shade said his name. The little rodent shot out from under the papers and stood on two hind legs. Shade noticed a red scarf around his neck. "Excellent! That is definitely good news to hear my friend. Good news indeed."

Shade lay down. "Okay?""

The mouse dusted himself off. "Excuse my arrogance, Shade. I'm a guest in your home at the moment, so I should be polite, not a pest, correct?"

Shade hesitated, and then nodded. This mouse's grammar was beginning to confuse him.

"Of course. Ahem, my name is Marvin, Marvin Mouse, to be accurate. You are Shade, one of the chosen, yes?"

"Yeah, I guess."

The mouse looked him up and down. "A bit scruffy to be chosen by the Sighters, I think."

Shade growled.

Marvin backed up. "Excuse me. That was terribly rude, I must say. Forgive me."

Shade gave a, *humph*, and nodded. "What are you here for anyways, Melvin?"

The mouse scowled at him. "*Marvin*. I have been sent by the Sighters to give you news of your quest. You will be on your next journey to collect the Fire Element in three days time."

Shade's jaw dropped. Three days?

"The Dark Lord has become much braver and more powerful. It won't be long before all of his Dark Forces attack our world. The elements are the only things that can save us." Marvin got back down on four paws.

Shade sighed. Why three days? Couldn't it be later?

Marvin passed his paws over his whiskers and twitched his nose. "I'd best be on my way. Good luck to you, Shade, and may you find peace at the end of your quest." With that, Marvin scurried around the left corner, out of sight.

Shade shook his head disapprovingly. That darn Dark Lord just wouldn't leave them alone! The Dark Lord was so intent on being the ruler of the world.

Why not run for president or something? Shade thought with a small laugh.

Just then, some dogs showed up. Five at least.

All led by Snag.

Shade gulped. This couldn't be good, could it? "Snag? Do you need something?"

Snag stalked up to Shade and leaned his face in. "Yeah I need something, you stupid trespassing idiot!"

Shade closed his eyes. Snag had said, 'trespassing': he knew that Shade had been there.

"Why in all of New York did I find *your* scent in *my* camp? Huh? Were you spying for all the other cowardly dogs in this city that didn't want to be part of my pack? Well?"

Shade kept his eyes closed. He didn't answer.

"Well?" Snag pried. "Why was your scent there? It didn't just… just *magically* appear there, did it? Do you really think I'm dumb enough to not recognize a dog's scent in my own camp? Do you?"

Shade swallowed hard. He hesitated before answering. His eyes remained closed. "No," he said in a small voice.

Snag started to shout. "Then why was your scent there, you mutt of a dog?"

Shade felt his muscles tense. "I don't know," he answered in a whisper.

"Excuse me?"

Shade spoke a bit louder. "I don't know."

Snag stepped closer his voice was so low that only Shade could hear him, none of the other five dogs he'd brought along. "*You don't know?*"

Shade began to tremble. He felt Snag's hot breath on his face. "No."

172

Snag growled deep in his throat. Shade dared to open his eyes. There was Snag, his unsightly, unkempt dark brown and gray face, only an inch away from his. His lips were peeled back in a more horrific snarl than Shade had ever seen. This dog cared a lot about his junkyard. "You. Are. Dead. Meat." His ears were pinned flat against his slicked back head fur.

Shade didn't move. He didn't speak. He barely breathed. He only stared into Snag's cruel amber eyes. "You were there. In my junkyard, my territory. Do you even understand borders? At *all?*"

Shade stayed still.

"I'm going to rip your flea-ridden throat out. You'll wish you were never born, wolf," Snag growled.

Deep inside of Shade, something clicked. *Wolf. Wolf...* Shade scrunched up his muzzle in a snarl. His eyes blazed with fury and power. He'd fought a raven; he'd encountered the ruler of all evil. Shade was strong enough to handle Snag. He stood up and squared his shoulders to look bigger. His back fur bristled. "You're right: I am a wolf," Shade said loud enough for Snag's gang to hear. "I've been through so much more than you have, Snag. You're the bad guy, not me. Not me at all."

Snag retreated his head. "Ha! As if."

Shade's claws scraped the pavement, making an eerie screeching noise. "Yeah. You're the one causing trouble. What did I ever do, huh? Not to mention, by the amount of hate that you have against me, why do you want me in your pack anyway? Do you just want to prove how strong you are? How powerful and mighty? Is that your goal? I *get* it, Snag. I *know* that you're the big one, the top dog. But you don't have to go imprisoning dogs to prove it. I know. Now leave me alone."

Snag let out a heart-stopping bark of anger. "That isn't why I'm here anyway, you stupid excuse for a dog! You were in my junkyard, and I want to know why."

Shade lowered his head. He stopped snarling, and his tail fell. "I was never there."

Snag leapt at Shade and barreled him over. "Yes you were! I even saw your silly bandana!"

Shade quickly drew his paws over his throat. He shut his eyes tightly. "Alright! Alright, alright! I was there, *I was there!*"

Snag barked in rage. "You admit it! Why? Why were you there? I swear, if you were spying I'll crush you!"

Shade yelped. "No! Why would I spy? I have no one to spy for!"

"Except yourself!"

Shade opened one eye. Saliva dripped from Snag's jaw, and his fangs glistened with menace. His eyes were wild and focused on Shade's face. His ears were pinned against his head. His tail stuck straight out, and a growl rumbled in his throat. His hind claws scored the asphalt, and the fur along his spine bristled in rage. "Why were you there, Half-mutt?"

Shade trembled as Snag tightened his grip along his sides. "Why were you there!"

"To find my sister!" Shade blurted out.

Snag loosened his grip and his eyes lost a bit of their wildness. "Your sister?"

"Yes!" Shade coughed and went on. "When you were here earlier I noticed her in your group. It took a second but then I realized who she was. I had to go find her, Snag. The only way to do that was to go into your camp, and I knew that if I actually tried asking you that you'd say no."

Snag tightened his grip again and creased his brow. "Of course I'd have said no! You would be an intruder in my territory. Bringing you in for a 'peek' would be a sign of weakness to the other pack members. You trespassed!"

Shade sighed as he realized that Snag still didn't understand. "You don't get it! She's my sister! I had to find her!"

Snag's gaze softened, and his eyes went a little misty, as though he was seeing a vision from the past. Perhaps he was remembering something. But the moment didn't last long, for Snag was immediately back to his normal, angry self. "Fine. You saw your sister. Happy?"

Shade nodded.

"Good." Snag shoved Shade forward, and his head slammed against the far wall. "Then stay out of my territory!" He grunted in

174

defiance. "I need you intact to be in my pack anyways." Snag turned around, and along with his gang, he disappeared. "We'll be back for you tomorrow," Shade heard him call from a distance.

Shade licked his lips. Snag was definitely not going to have him.

Chapter 42

Hurricane hung his head as Stormy jabbered away at Fletch. The club leader looked alarmed, and an expression of disapproval consumed his face as he turned to meet Hurricane's eyes. "Hurricane, is all of this true?"

Hurricane glanced to his side where Lexie stood a few inches from the edge of the shelf. Fletch was sitting on a red towel with lanterns on either side. At the other end of the towel was the wall. A Guard stood on either side of Hurricane as he stood on a sheet of tinfoil, the spot where cats took their place if they wished to speak with Fletch. Stormy obviously didn't care about being formal at the moment, so he was standing right in front of Fletch's face, the tips of his paws touching the red trim of Fletch's towel throne.

"I... uh..." Hurricane stuttered.

"Speak!" Stormy snapped. One of the Guards lifted a paw as a signal for Stormy to stay calm and be quiet. Stormy grunted.

"Y-yes. It's all true."

The Guards shook their heads in pity. Hurricane wanted to whip around and break their Guard Chains right off their necks. Official Guards wore special chains around their necks to symbolize that they are Guards. Lexie's tail drooped.

"Well, I'm not going to end this meeting without hearing your side of the story. Any good leader would listen to both sides."

Hurricane was surprised and a bit relieved. Maybe he wouldn't have to go to the crate after all. "Well, uh, you see, I-"

Stormy cut him off. "Forget his side of the story! What about *my* side? What about the danger that *my* kitten was put in?"

Fletch dipped his head. "Hurricane's side is just as important as yours, Stormy. Let the cat speak."

Hurricane lifted his head. "Well, um, I woke up this morning, really early. Yeah, and, uh, Rainy came over to me, see? She started bombarding me with the same question over and over again: 'can I go outside?' Well she wouldn't leave me alone, and I expected that no matter how many times I said no, she'd probably just sneak out anyway. So, instead of her sneaking out without anyone watching her, I decided to just take her with me. So I had two options: have her outside with me and watch her, or having her outside with me without knowing she was there. Which would you choose?"

Fletch was nodding slowly. The Guards looked confused, but Stormy's expression was obvious: intense anger. "That's not an excuse!" he roared.

Hurricane flinched back and stole a look at Lexie. Her face looked frightened. Hurricane mouthed the word '*great*'. Lexie flicked her tail.

"Well..." Fletch considered.

"He broke the rules! You shouldn't even be considering letting him have this argument! I won't stand for it!"

Hurricane's mouth opened a bit in surprise. This tom was fiercely protective of his kittens.

Fletch even looked surprised. "Look Stormy, if you calm down, then maybe I'll come to an actual conclusion."

Stormy, with the order of one of the Guards, sat down, his gray pelt rippling in frustration.

"Okay. Let's look at the facts. Hurricane was, in a way, forced to let Rainy outside." Fletch gave a small grin as he tried to hold in a laugh. "Although, Stormy has brought forth the law, which is something that none of us can really argue with. No, I will not change the law for this one predicament. But then, perhaps I could make an exception..."

Stormy's mouth gaped in shock. Hurricane's ears pricked at the thought of being let off the hook.

"Since Hurricane needs to speak to the club about his disappearance, and a convict is not welcome to speak to a crowd. Therefore, I will let you go this once."

Hurricane's jaw went slack with amazement. His eyes widened, and his tail waved happily. "Thank you, Fletch!" Hurricane turned his gaze to the bristling bulk of Stormy. "I'm sorry for putting your daughter in danger. I should have gotten your permission. Please accept my apologies?"

Stormy snarled, nodding against his will. With one last angry glare at Fletch, he leaped onto the plank of wood that acted as a stairway to Fletch's home. Hurricane sighed in relief.

Lexie padded up to him. "You are an absolute idiot." She gave him a friendly shove.

Hurricane smiled. "Oh don't worry, I know."

Chapter 43

Hurricane couldn't stand still. He was worried. Very worried. What would he say? He couldn't tell the club about the Dark Forces, not yet. He would have to make something up. He had barely given his speech any thought, and now it was time to reveal the reason for his absence of three whole days.

"Now, if you will all quiet down, Hurricane will tell you all of his journey," Hurricane heard Fletch say from behind the Stage Crate. The Stage Crate was where cats made speeches to the club. They stood on top of the crate and said what they had to say. Fletch hopped down and went behind the box to where Hurricane sat trembling. "You're on," he declared. "Good luck." With that, he leapt back on top of the Stage Crate and sat, waiting for Hurricane to appear beside him.

Hurricane hesitated. He was still unsure of what to say. He decided that he would do his best, and jumped up. His eyes skimmed the huge crowd, looking for one cat in particular. Ah, there she was. Lexie sat huddled against her brother, Vixen. Hurricane gulped.

"Well, I'm sure that all of you are wondering why I was gone, yes?" The crowd muttered in reply. "Of course. Why I was gone..." *What do I say?* "You see, uh, I was hunting and..." *yeah, let's start there.* "I dumpster-dove and, well, I met... I met... a cat. Yes, a cat. The cat's name was, um, Dapple. Yeah, Dapple." Hurricane was gaining confidence. A scene unfolded in his mind, and he created an adventurous story. He went on about how this "Dapple" was a wild cat who lived in the forest at the edge of the city. She had a litter of kittens and her mate had left her. Hurricane said that he had seen that she needed help by the fact that he could see her ribs, and she looked as though she had a cold. So, he followed her to where she lived. She had told him that foxes and dogs invaded the woods often, and that she needed him to help her move her kittens to a safer place. So for three days, the two of them searched for the best place to live, since she refused to live anywhere outside the forest. She was a wild cat, she had insisted. Finally, the two found the perfect spot, and with Hurricane's help, she settled in. The prey was plentiful in the new area, and there were no predators to be seen or scented. Then, Hurricane came home. The end.

The crowd cheered for Hurricane's heroism, and were all relieved that the made-up she-cat had found a good home. Hurricane was glad that they believed it, but he was a bit disconcerted by the fact that he had just lied to everyone he knew.

Hurricane jumped off of the crate and shifted through the crowd. Many cats stopped him to congratulate his thoughtfulness to "Dapple". He wondered if he would ever tell them that it was just a story. Perhaps he would, one day.

Hurricane padded over to the food-stock and grabbed a piece of bread. He chewed it slowly, relishing its softness. With a gulp, Hurricane left through the entrance. He was met once again by Buck and Spur.

"What's new, Pussy-Cat?" Buck sang. "Whoa, whoa-*whoa*-oh!" He burst into laughter at his own joke. "So, where're you going, smart-one?"

Hurricane lashed his tail. Spur sat quietly still, watching Hurricane with a wary look. The poor, shy little tom. He was trying to be a Guard, at least. "Hunting. It's nerve-racking on stage."

Buck spat on the ground. Hurricane and Spur cringed. "Grab somethin' good."

Hurricane snorted. "'Kay." He trotted off, his tail swinging behind him rhythmically. Soon, he came upon a ripped open trash bag. He dug his nose into it, not giving his actions much thought.

Then he smelled something odd. It was cat, but not any cat he knew. He sniffed the bag and sneezed. Strays.

Hurricane looked left and right. The scent was fresh; too fresh. He began to back away from the bag. When it comes to food, cats with no groups can be violent. Hurricane lived in a society where there were laws and organization, but some strays live in small duos or trios without rules. Cats like that fight with no thought, only blind rage. They could be vicious and dangerous, especially at night. Darkness is their weapon; they use it as a wide hiding place. Though, their lack of tactics can prove to be a downfall. With no plan, no specific techniques, a vicious stray could be overcome by a cat that does use those tools. The club called group-less, violent strays like these Snatchers.

Just as Hurricane was spinning around to sprint away, he collided with the giant bulk of a tom. He stared blankly into the face of the foe, whose eyes burned with satisfaction. "What'syer name?"

Hurricane opened his mouth to reply, but nothing came out.

"Talk, idiot." The tom's mottled brown and black pelt rippled with power from the muscles beneath. His two companions, a black tom with gray paws and a mud-brown tom with a tan belly, growled a threat.

Hurricane swallowed, and spoke. "Hurricane."

The Snatchers laughed. "What sort'a messed up name is that?" the lead Snatcher cackled.

Hurricane tensed. "What's wrong with my name?"

"It's a big name for a little guy," the Snatcher declared.

"Then what's your name, big guy?"

The Snatcher narrowed his gaze. "Hook. These here are my gang." Hook, clearly the leader now, motioned to the black, gray-pawed tom. "That there's Talon," he pointed to the mud-colored tom, "and that's Pierce."

Hurricane lashed his tail. "You all obviously think of yourselves as tough."

Hook hissed. "We're sure that."

Hurricane avoided his gaze. "Let me go."

Hook lowered his head with a hiss. "I don't know…"

"Let's get 'im!" Pierce spat. "It'll be good exercise, Hook."

"Yeah, Hook. Let's give him a beating he won't forget."

Hook hissed at his gang. "I make the decisions, you hear?" Hook turned back to Hurricane. Looking resentful, he hesitated before saying, "I'll let you off this time. But don't steal our food again."

Hurricane couldn't believe his ears. "Th-thank you."

Hook yowled in annoyance. "Scat!"

Hurricane jumped and took off running. He could hardly believe his luck. A gang of Snatchers had literally just let him go without a scratch. *This was supposed to be a walk that would calm me down, not shake me up.*

Hurricane slipped into a quiet, vacant alley and tried to push over a trashcan. The can wouldn't budge, but in the corner he found another bag. Approaching it cautiously, sniffing the air at the same time, he advanced on the plastic bag. No cat scent; it smelled only of stale human. He sighed relief and ripped open the bag with a swift claw. Old meat spilled out. Hurricane wrinkled his nose in disgust. That wasn't edible.

Hurricane ran away from the offending odor and into the nearby park. He would hunt, and bring back a reasonable meal.

Chapter 44

Shade paced over the soft beach sand. Today was the day that Snag would come to collect him. He had decided to flee to the sandy shore that overlooked the Atlantic Ocean. He would wait here. He would refuse to be taken away.

Minutes passed. Shade had resorted to lying under a cabana porch overhang. He sat silently as humans constantly trotted up, asking for a drink or food. Shade was amazed that any humans had even come today. It was late autumn, and they were in New York City. Humans had no fur to armor themselves against the cold. They wore bulky, uncomfortable-looking coats in the cold season. They could not bear the below-freezing temperatures on their own.

Minutes morphed into hours. Shade found himself dozing in and out of sleep. The pattering of feet decreased to a few stragglers who had decided to watch the sun set over the ocean. Shade was baffled as to how they expected to do this; thick wintry clouds covered the sky like a gray blanket. Every day now seemed to be overcast. Shade didn't complain though. He personally liked cloudy days. They were dark and quiet. Though, he preferred the skies to be clear during the night. Shade enjoyed gazing at the twinkling stars above.

Finally, the last few small groups left the eastern shoreline. Casinos and restaurants had turned on their bright, colorful lights, which lit up the beach. Shade finally squeezed out from under the cabana. He had only left the little hut once or twice to eat something. He had easily done so by pulling a half-eaten something off of one of the tables. He dragged the leftover food under the porch and ate.

Shade's legs and back were sore. He stretched joyously outside on the sand. He had just slept the day away. He was now full of energy. He felt as though he could run to one end of the east coast and back. A bolt of energy seared through him, sending a shiver running up his back. Excitement sent a chill through him and he went racing forward. He ran until he tripped over a heap of sand and toppled to the ground. But the energy streak did not cease. Shade rolled over and over in the sand, feeling some itches along his back disappear. He sprang up and began digging, throwing up dirt behind himself. He gave a jubilant leap into the air and repeated the entire process. Finally, he no longer felt the chills running up his spine or the energy that pulsed in his veins. His muscles relaxed, and he let the tenseness of his limbs go. Shade plopped down on his side, panting hard to the rhythm of his heartbeat.

Shade's aching soreness left his muscles and he stood up. He shook out his fur of the sand that clung to it and licked some stubborn spots away. Finally, he was ready to head back.

*   *   *   *   *   *   *   *

After a time of walking, Shade came upon his alley. The mutt fell happily into his bed and curled up. But something smelled. Shade's head popped up to sniff the air. A scent lingered there, both stale and fresh. The scent was obvious: Snag. Shade stood up and shuffled around his den. Some of Snag's scent was stale while others were quite fresh. The dog must have come once that day and seen that Shade was not there. Then he probably sent little Pick-Up Patrols to check whether or not the wolf had come back. Shade sat down in his nest. What if Snag came tomorrow, too? Would he just hide on the beach again?

Shade circled three or four times and laid down. The scent hung around him like a cloud threatening to storm. He managed to sleep silently, but images of Snag's enraged face whirled throughout his dreams.

Chapter 45

Hurricane stood outside, gazing up at the stars. Two days had passed. Tomorrow was the day that he and Shade would search for the next element, Fire. He felt that this time, finding the element would be different.

Suddenly, a cat appeared at his side. Hurricane jumped and peered at the cat through the darkness. It was Lexie. "Hurricane, could I ask you something?"

Hurricane nodded. "Sure."

"Is everything that Rainy said true?"

Her question shot through him like lightning. "What?"

"I said, 'is everything that Rainy said true?'"

Hurricane looked at his paws. Should he tell her?

"Hurricane?"

Hurricane swallowed back a cry. "Y-yes…"

Lexie's eyes shot wider. "'Wait, what?"

Hurricane sprang to his paws. He could hold the secret no longer. "Yes! Yes! It's all true, every last bit! I've been chosen to save the world!"

Lexie backed away from him. "Hurricane…"

"Don't walk away! I can't stand it any longer! No, I wasn't gone for three days helping some cat! I was captured! And tortured! I've been through more than any cat could imagine! I've faced death!"

Lexie stopped backing up. "Hurricane, I think you might need some help."

"No! It's the truth! Do you wonder why I leave for such long periods of time? It's because I'm on some stupid quest that I've been forced into! I didn't ask for the weight of the whole world's safety to be put on my shoulders, but I got it! I get to save everyone from darkness!"

Lexie started to sit down. She closed her eyes. "Slow down Hurricane. Tell me everything. You have someone to talk to, don't worry."

Hurricane was panting. He shook with frustration at his responsibilities. Why had he been chosen? He was nobody. He was just another stray cat in the city. Hurricane began with how he met Shade, who back then was only a stubborn mutt who wouldn't leave him alone. He got to the part about the abandoned house and Everest. He told her Everest's words, of their destiny to save the planet from the Dark Lord. He told her of the quests that they were sent on, and of the desperation to keep all of it a secret.

When Hurricane finished, he heaved a great sigh. It felt as though a huge weight had been lifted off of his shoulders. Lexie shook her head. "No, you're not serious."

Hurricane had to make her believe it. "It's true. It's all true."

Lexie gazed into his eyes. "Prove it."

Hurricane grabbed the scruff of her neck. "I will." He dragged her forward a bit. Lexie pulled away.

"Hurricane! Stop! That hurts!"

Hurricane winced. Lexie had done nothing wrong, yet he was taking his anger out on her. "Sorry." Hurricane motioned for her to follow him. "This way."

Lexie stood still. "No."

Hurricane's tail drooped. "Please?"

Lexie turned her head away. "Don't drag me like that again. I don't know what's gotten into you?"

Hurricane shuffled his paws. "I won't."

Lexie gave in. "Fine then. Convince me."

Hurricane motioned to the same direction. "Then what are you waiting for?' He walked forward, Lexie tagging along with him. After a few minutes, Shade's alley came into sight.

Lexie bristled, but said nothing. Hurricane padded on and slipped around the corner. There was Shade, lying in his nest. *Good.*

Hurricane prodded Shade with a paw. Shade's head rose slowly. The wolf yawned. "Wha...?"

"Shade. I need you to do something for me."

Shade yawned. "Hurricane? Is that you?"

"Yeah."

"Okay, what?" Shade turned from his side to a Sphinx-like position.

Hurricane nodded at Lexie. "I told her."

Shade leapt out of bed. He leaned his face into Hurricane's. "You did what?"

Hurricane gulped. He hadn't expected this reaction. "I told her."

"Everything?" Hurricane said nothing. "Hurricane, why?"

"She asked."

"What?"

"A kitten from where I live spilled the news. She asked if it was true." Hurricane closed his eyes, waiting for Shade to do something horrible. He'd seen his wolf side come out before. He swallowed hard.

"I told someone too," Shade finally admitted.

Hurricane opened his eyes. "You did?"

Shade nodded. "My sister."

"You have a sister?"

"I didn't even know up until a few days ago." Hurricane tilted his head. "It's a long story."

Hurricane shook his head. "Whatever. Just tell her. It's all true, isn't it?"

Shade glared at Lexie. "Yes."

Lexie gaped at him. "It is?"

Hurricane and Shade nodded simultaneously. "So… some evil dragon guy is trying to take over the world?"

When she put it like that, it sounded hilarious. "Um, yeah."

Lexie trembled. "What if you don't find all of the elements in time?"

"We're going to find the last one tomorrow."

Lexie sighed. "Wow."

Hurricane coughed. "Yeah. In fact, Shade and I should probably talk it over."

Lexie flicked her tail. "Okay." She didn't leave. Hurricane and Shade glanced at each other uncomfortably. "Well?"

"Um…" Shade woofed.

"Should I leave?" Lexie asked, lowering her head.

"Probably."

Lexie closed her eyes. "Okay. I'll see you at the club, Hurricane." Lexie cantered around the corner, out of sight. Her paw-steps faded into the distance.

"Okay. So when do we leave?"

Shade's ears perked up. "It's only three in the morning. Why are we talking about leaving now?"

"Has Marvin visited you?"

Shade cocked his head. "Yeah. Why?"

Hurricane rolled his eyes. "Didn't you hear what he said?"

"All I remember is his grammar obsession."

"Through the grammar!"

Shade thought. "Just tell me."

Hurricane bristled. "That Than is getting stronger!"

Shade sat down and narrowed his eyes. His face had a confused expression. "Who's Than?"

"That's the Dark Lord's name. He was called Than before he became the high king of darkness."

Shade sighed. "You learned a lot while you were captured, huh?"

Hurricane gave a weak smile. "Yeah. I even learned about the ranks and stuff."

Shade made a sweeping motion with his paws, imitating shooing away a fly. "Whatever. All I care about is whether you learned any valuable information. Did you?"

"Of course I did. Like, the fact that only dragons can become the Dark Lord, that there are ten command positions, you know, stuff like that."

"But how does that help us defeat the Dark Forces?"

"It doesn't! Shade, all that matters is whether or not we can find the four elements. Then we're home free!"

Shade nodded. "Okay, okay. I get it. So, should we leave now?"

Hurricane looked into Shade's eyes with uncertainty. "Yeah. Yeah, we should!" Hurricane turned and walked toward the edge of the alley. "Let's go."

*   *   *   *   *   *   *   *   *

The abandoned house loomed before them, vacant and gloomy. The porch sagged on its flimsy stilts, and the wood creaked eerily. An old swing hung from a tree and was being pushed by the wind. Hurricane shuddered. It looked creepy. Suddenly, there was a crack, and some wood snapped off of the house, followed by a handful of tumbling rocks. The two chosen ones gulped.

The wolf and cat squeezed through the permanently ajar door. The floor creaked and screeched, as though it were crying out. Hurricane felt a splinter penetrate through his pad. With a yelp, he sat down to work it out of his paw. He hated every minute of this.

Shade looked down at the tom. "What's up?"

Hurricane hissed in annoyance. "I got a splinter!"

Shade blew a piece of hair that had been hanging in front of his face out of the way. "Whines the cat who fought a raven."

"Shut up," Hurricane growled as he tried to pry the splinter out of his paw with his teeth.

Shade laughed and sat down patiently as his quest partner growled and yanked at his pad. Hurricane was constantly cursing about the pain. "It hurts!"

Shade grinned, his eyes reflecting laughter. "I know. I'd help, but while I tried I'd probably bite your paw off by accident." Hurricane only hissed in reply. "Lots of drama over a splinter." He snapped his head forward and nipped Shade's flank. "Ow!"

The two heard a creaking noise behind them. They were both still a bit scared from when they first walked into the spooky house a few minutes ago, so the noise made them jump. Shade stood up and walked in front of Hurricane. "Who's there?"

Hurricane growled. "I can protect myself!"

Shade moaned as Hurricane stood up, wincing from his "injured" paw. "Answer!" Shade barked.

A figure stepped out of the shadows. Shade was about to swoop down and grab Hurricane by the scruff, but stopped. The two sighed in relief as Everest revealed himself to them. "Hello, youngsters."

Hurricane shook the fear out of his pelt. "Hi, Everest."

Everest nodded in greeting. "Hello. Why are you two here so early?"

"We're going to find the final element. We decided to get it done early."

Everest gave a chuckle. "You two act like this is just a job."

"It's beginning to feel like it." Shade sat and flicked an ear. "I met a talking mouse named Marvin and was barely fazed."

190

"Yeah. We're getting used to it." Hurricane licked a paw.

Everest smiled. "Good then. Enough chit-chat. Let's finish this quest once and for all." The usual flash of light blinded the two of them, and all three were sent spiraling into another world.

Chapter 46

When the light cleared, Shade and Hurricane were surprised to see Everest still with them. "Everest? What are you doing here? You never come with us."

"I know. But first, we stop at the Rocky Mountain Sighter Meeting."

Hurricane and Shade looked at each other with a mix of surprise and excitement. "Didn't you say that Sighter Cats would be here, too?" Hurricane asked.

Everest nodded, smiling. "Come with me." He motioned to a cave.

Shade shivered. "It's cold."

"Well, duh. We're in the Rockies," Hurricane pointed out.

Shade stuck out his tongue in mock annoyance. Hurricane could be pushy. "Come on."

Once they had entered, Shade and Hurricane froze in awe. The entire place was ice; ice ceiling, ice floor, ice walls, even a stage area made completely of ice. Ice stalactites hung from the cave ceiling, and stalagmites created small areas on the ground where Sighter Cats and Dogs chatted. Huge ice columns stretched from the ground to the top of the giant cave dome. Some smaller cats and dogs were running around the ice stage, preparing for some sort of performance.

"Are they reciting the reenactment?" Shade asked.

"Yes," Everest replied, looking in another direction. Shade followed his gaze. When he saw where Everest was looking, he was astonished. There was Klondike, much older now. Everest smiled and raced over to his old mentor. Shade and Hurricane followed.

"Shade, Hurricane, meet my old mentor, Klondike. She trained me." Everest looked at his old mentor with excitement glowing in his eyes. "I only get to see other Sighters at this meeting."

Shade bowed his head in respect, but was bewildered when Klondike, and all the other dogs around her, bowed to him and Hurricane instead. "The chosen ones," they said formally. When they lifted their heads, a group of students galloped over.

"Are you the chosen ones?" "Are you really going to save the world?" "Why are you half wolf?" "Air told us that she dropped you on top of a raven!" The questions kept coming.

One of the Sighters stomped up to the students. "Quit it!" The pups and kittens scattered.

Everest leaned toward the wolf and cat. "That's K2. He never exactly wanted to be a Sighter, but he went with it."

K2's face twisted with annoyance, and he went back to talking to a light brown dog. "Obviously, he isn't cut out for the job."

"That's not completely true," Everest protested. "Yes, we would rather he be more peaceful, but he does well with interpreting signs."

Shade wasn't convinced, but said nothing more.

Hurricane got Everest's attention with a prodding paw. "Can I go meet the Sighter Cats?"

Everest looked over to where a crowd of cats, surrounded by a circle of ice stalagmites, sat talking. Their feathers swished as they laughed. "Sure. Just be respectful." Hurricane nodded eagerly and bounced over. Shade stayed beside Everest with the other dogs.

"Hi, there!" Hurricane mewed, his Air Pouch swaying.

"Ah, the chosen one!" a gray cat with black stripes trilled. "Hello, Hurricane."

Hurricane grinned. "What's your name?"

"Aries," the tom replied.

"Cool!" Hurricane turned to the other five cats. "What are your names?"

Going in a circle, the cats answered. "I'm Sagittarius," a black tom answered.

"I'm Orion," a blue-gray tom declared.

"I'm Scorpio," said a reddish she-cat.

"Leo," said a golden tom simply.

"I'm Virgo!" said a younger silver she-cat excitedly. "I just finished my training."

Hurricane waved his tail happily. "Congrats!"

As Hurricane spoke to the Sighter Cats, Shade went on chatting with the Sighter Dogs. "So when does the news exchange begin?"

"In time, Shade," a dog known as Fuji repeated. "In time."

Everest looked outside to the rising sun. "It won't be long now."

"How long does the Sighter Festival last?" Shade asked.

"The whole day. But we won't stay forever. You two will need to be off soon."

"You're leaving so soon?" a Sighter known as Doan asked.

"Yes. They must find the last element."

"Oh, of course!" Doan nodded in understanding. "You should be going soon."

Shade felt a bit disappointed, but didn't argue. Instead, he asked something else. "When does the reenactment happen?"

"When the sun sets," Everest answered.

Shade's ears drooped. "Oh."

Everest smiled a bit sadly. "Sorry. Maybe next year."

Shade blinked. "Next year?"

Everest seemed to catch himself. "Why yes."

Shade beamed. "Okay!"

Suddenly, a blazing orange light lit up the ice cave. Shade looked out the entrance. There was the morning sun, peeking over the mountains, it's light shining like fire in the cave. Many of the dogs and cats gave out sighs of awe, as did Shade. What a beautiful sight.

Hurricane shuffled up beside Shade. "Wow."

Shade sighed and let himself slump. The sight made him sleepy.

"Sighters of the world!" A voice boomed. Shade turned to see a powerful-looking dog standing on the stage. "It is time for the news exchange to begin!"

Shade leaned over to Everest. "Who's that?"

"That's Rocky. He's the leader of all the Sighter Dogs. His father was the leader before he died, as was his father before him, before him, before *him*, and so on. The position of leader is passed on to the former leader's pup when they die."

"Are she-dogs ever leader?"

"Oh, yes, of course. It's not as though there's a law against it. It's just that for some reason the leader's pup never turns out to be a girl."

"Why?" Shade persisted.

"Nobody knows," Everest answered vaguely. "Come on." Everest walked toward the ice stage. Shade followed. The two sat down near the back.

Hurricane padded after the two of them. "Where's the Sighter Cat leader?"

Everest pointed with his nose at a she-cat with an unusual orange and silver pelt. "That's Aurora."

"It's not a constellation name," Hurricane pointed out.

"Yes, you're right. But all Sighter Cat leaders are named Aurora. That's a question you could ask the Sighter Cats if you're interested enough." Hurricane licked his lips and focused on Rocky.

"Sighters of cats and dogs alike! We are gathered here today for the annual meeting of the Winter Solstice. I understand that the Sighter Cats are a bit unsatisfied at the fact that they must have their meeting at the ancient site of Sighter Dog meetings, but please be forgiving. We must all gather together somewhere to discuss our main topic of distress: the Dark Forces."

Every Sighter in the crowd began muttering and whining at the mention of their foe. It was obviously troubling them that the Dark Lord was becoming so bold.

"Fear not!" Rocky reassured. "For the chosen ones have come!"

Shade and Hurricane felt as though a huge weight had been put on their shoulders. The crowd cheered for them. "The chosen ones! The chosen ones!"

Shade gave a forced smile, as did Hurricane. The two of them were glancing back and forth at each other with uncertain expressions.

They were the chosen ones.

Chapter 47

Shade and Hurricane listened to a long rambling from Rocky about how awful the Dark Lord is, and then leaned forward as Aurora stepped up to take his place. She was young and pretty, probably new to being leader just as Rocky was. "Everyone! Tonight we are united and come together as one. Not as cats and dogs, but as Sighters and Sighters alone. We shall cherish this day of peace between the two species. In any event, let us give thanks to Rocky and the Sighter Dogs for offering their ancient place of meeting to us so that we could all gather together." Aurora turned from the crowd to nod at Rocky in thanks, and many of the Sighter Cats muttered their own. Aurora turned back to the crowd. "We stand against a powerful opponent. The Dark Lord knows no boundaries, and will go beyond the worst to get what he wants. He has chosen to walk a dark path with his shadowy army, and plots against us. But we will fight, and we will fight as one." She turned her gaze to Shade and Hurricane. Hurricane felt claws of anxiety prick his pelt as her gaze bore into his. She had one amber eye and one blue, like fire and ice searing through him.

"The two saviors have been chosen, and they do their best to save us on their seemingly endless quest." *She's got that right.* Hurricane thought. "But they will pull through, for they were chosen judging by the signs from wind, pebble and water. We have watched the world around us and have interpreted the signs. These two will save us."

Hurricane heaved a sigh. They kept going on and on about how he and Shade would save them. The question was: would they? Hurricane pondered over this for a moment before being roused by Everest.

"Time to go, young one. I will accompany you on your fourth and final quest. Come." Everest motioned towards the cave entrance. Hurricane and Shade followed. Once they were outside, Everest turned to them. "Before we leave, I want you both to know that you have done an exceptional job. All that I have seen from you is beyond what I expected. Before this, you were two strays, traipsing about the city, only worried about where to sleep or where you'd find your next meal. You were stripped off the streets by a prophecy, and you allowed yourselves to be brought into the center of this chaotic journey to save all you know. That, my friends, is courage."

Hurricane's sight began to wither. A black cloud obscured his vision. When he could see no more, a shockwave of bravery shot up his spine like lightning. He would do whatever it took to save his friends, his family, and his world.

*   *   *   *   *   *   *   *   *

Hurricane found himself lying among the sharp edges of gray and black rocks that surrounded a huge mountain with a flat top. Or was it a mountain? "Is that... is that a volcano?" Hurricane asked.

Everest, lying on his side as well as Shade, turned his head toward the huge landform. "Yes," he said simply.

Hurricane gulped. "Will we go inside?"

Everest hesitated before nodding. "Yes."

Chapter 48

Shade followed Everest up the rocky slope with Hurricane at his heels. "My paws are bleeding," Hurricane complained.

Shade began to limp. Small red trickles appeared on the ground where he stepped. "Mine too."

Everest stopped and turned to them. "Want to take a break?" Hurricane and Shade plopped down on their bellies as an answer. "Well then, a break it is." Everest circled a few times and laid down under a scraggly shrub with no leaves. "My paws hurt too."

Shade looked at his own paws. "Are yours bleeding?"

Everest looked. "No."

"I hate to break up such an interesting conversation," Hurricane began sarcastically, "but how on Earth do we get inside the volcano? It's not like we can go in through the top. We'd fall."

Everest closed his eyes. "There is a small cave entrance in the side of it. We will go in through there."

Shade nodded and closed his eyes, allowing sleep to take him in.

When Shade woke up, it was at least 2:00 pm. He shoved Hurricane in the side. "Wake up, lazy-bones. It's past noon."

Hurricane woke with a start. He checked his pads. "They're not bleeding anymore."

"Congrats. Now let's go." Shade tickled Hurricane's nose with his tail to rouse him.

"Quit it!" yowled Hurricane with a sneeze, succeeding in waking up Everest.

"Wha...?" Everest yawned. "Are you two ready to get moving now?"

"Everest, it's past noon," Shade pointed out.

Everest sprang to his paws. "Past noon? Then what are you waiting for? Come on!" Everest bounded up the path, his red feather flying out from behind his ear. Hurricane grabbed the cardinal feather in his teeth and followed Everest.

"Everest?" the tom said through clenched teeth. "You dropped something."

Everest turned to Hurricane. "My feather! Thank you, Hurricane." Everest leaned his head down as Hurricane struggled to twine the feather through his fur.

"There. It'll be while before it falls out again. I tied it onto your fur pretty well."

"Good. Very good. Come, we have a quest to finish." Everest, walking slower now, proceeded up the slope.

"For an old dog, he's got some spunk," Hurricane commented.

Everest continued to lead the way up the path, but the hard pointed rocks made walking hard for Shade and Hurricane. They had really only ever walked up and down flat asphalt streets, which of course were nothing like this. Shade struggled to keep up, but the cuts in his pads were slowing him down. Everest, being a descendant from ancient mountain dogs, was used to such rough terrain.

"Are we almost there?" Hurricane moaned as a few more minutes passed.

"Yes," Everest answered patiently. "Nearly."

Hurricane sighed relief. Shade couldn't blame him. Suddenly, a few black pebbles rolled out from behind a boulder. Everest stepped in front of the two of them. "Stay still," he instructed. Hurricane and Shade obeyed. More tumbling of rocks and more shuffling noises followed. Then, from behind the boulder bounced a puppy.

"Hi! I'm Bandit," yipped the tiny golden ball of fluff. "I'm a Golden Retriever!'

Everest stepped aside for the two to see. "Hi," Hurricane meowed.

Bandit was bouncing circles around the trio. "I'm your guide! Are you excited? Because I'm excited! I'm Bandit! I'm going to help you find Fire in that *big* volcano and I'm your guide! I-"

"Slow down, hotrod. You're starting to repeat stuff." Hurricane lifted a paw as a sign to stop.

"Sorry! I'm just so excited to be helping you guys on your quest and it's so great and... and... just wow!"

"Fun," Shade commented.

"Come on!" Bandit spun around and dashed up the slope. The three followed at a steadier pace, but kept their guide in sight. An hour passed with the same process replaying itself over and over. Bandit would run ahead for a bit, get tired, and fall back to where the other three trotted rhythmically. He would catch his breath, go on about dozens of different random things, and then sprint ahead again. Then the process would repeat.

"Don't you ever get tired?" Shade asked when Bandit would fall back after a bit. "Enough to have to stop completely?"

"Rarely!" Bandit declared. "There's too much to see and do to be tired!" Bandit gave a little bounce. "'Enjoy life while you still can,' that's my motto!"

Hurricane stopped and smiled. This puppy had a point. Shade leaned down to Bandit's face. "That's a very good motto to have," he said. Bandit beamed, and ran in a happy circle.

Hurricane leaned over to Shade. "Were *you* ever that hyper?"

Shade shrugged. He was never very good at remembering that far back. "Maybe."

Hurricane cocked his head, and averted his gaze. "Hey Everest, won't fire burn our pouches?"

Shade rolled his eyes, but the unusually patient Everest simply answered Hurricane's obvious question. "It is a special kind of pouch. Magic, Hurricane, magic."

"'Kay," Hurricane replied.

"There!" Bandit piped. "Right there! Do you see it? The cave's right there!"

Everest put a paw on the pup's back. "We see it, we see it. Calm down." Bandit gave an excited yip and shot forward.

"Follow me!" he hooted. The little fluffy bundle disappeared inside.

"Let's follow him before he falls in a pit of lava," Hurricane moaned.

When the group walked in, they gaped at the sight. The opening in the volcano presented itself what seemed to be miles above. The walls of the volcano were mixtures of browns and tans. A pool of magma bubbled in a moat around an island of brown rock. A narrow rock path made a bridge to the small island. In the center of the island stood a tall stalagmite, and levitating above it, an orange globe. Inside the globe, flames licked the sides, but did not burn it. "I'm glad I don't have to wear a pouch full of fire around *my* neck," Shade smirked jokingly.

"Oh, shut up," Hurricane replied laughingly.

"Come," Everest ordered. He began walking across the brown rock bridge.

Hurricane gave a "Ha!" as though he'd never heard anything so ridiculous. "You expect me to walk across *that?*"

Shade groaned and grabbed Hurricane by his scruff. He wasn't crazy about the thought of walking across a bridge that went over *lava*, but they would have to at some point. "Hey! Put me down!" Hurricane squirmed in Shade's grasp. Once they were in the middle of the bridge, Shade set him free. "What was that for?"

"You wouldn't have moved. I gave you a boost."

"Some boost!" Hurricane protested. Shade rolled his eyes, but jumped straight up in the air when a bubble of lava popped. Hurricane did the same.

"Come on you two!" Bandit shot past them, skidding to a halt when he reached the island.

Hurricane and Shade looked at each other. "If a puppy can do it, so can we," Shade declared.

202

Hurricane trotted quickly after Shade and let out a relieved sigh as his paws met the island. There was the final element, floating while making a quiet *whirring* noise. They could hear the crackling of the fire through the globe.

A burst of flames sent every head turning away. There, in all her beauty, stood the keeper of the Fire Element. She was bright orange, the color of flame. Her tail was shaped like a blaze. From her paws sprouted tiny flames. One eye was amber, and the other was yellow. An orange glow surrounded her figure. The she-cat dipped her head in greeting. "Welcome. I am Fire, keeper of the fourth element."

Hurricane's jaw dropped. Everest bowed his head in greeting. "Hello, Fire. I am honored to be in your presence."

Shade blinked. The other keepers had looked interesting, but none of them had fire coming out of their paws! Though, he still thought that Air succeeded in getting first place with her wings.

"Now, Hurricane, say the words, and possess the element. Hurry!"
Hurricane climbed the stalagmite and reached a paw towards the globe. He looked around. No sign of the Dark Forces. That was strange. If they were ever to come, it would most likely be now, when their quest is nearly finished. But no one was there.

"Fire, the fourth element," Hurricane recited. The globe dropped into his outstretched paw. Still no Dark Forces in sight.

"Keep going," Shade insisted.

Hurricane pressed against the globe with his paws. It disappeared. At first, Hurricane expected searing pain to shoot through his paws from the heat, but it did not. The flames still flickered in his grasp, but there was no pain. He looked at Everest in confusion.

"Magic," was all Everest said. Hurricane nodded and took the flames, surprisingly, in his teeth.

"I don't get it," Hurricane said through clenched teeth. "We could hold air, water, and now fire, all in our *teeth*. Do scientific laws just not go for any of this?"

Everest only laughed. Bandit bounced up and tied an orange pouch around Hurricane's neck. He took the element and plopped it in the Fire Pouch.

Hurricane and Shade's pouches began to glow. They got brighter and brighter until the entire area was nothing but blazing light.

Chapter 49

There they were, in the middle of a windy vacant street. Newspapers and trash twirled across the sidewalks like tumbleweeds.

"Are we back in New York?" Shade asked.

Everest nodded. "The elements can only be activated in the real world."

Shade creased his brow. "Why?"

"A law of magic. Only a Sighter can activate them - that's where I come in."

Hurricane paced. "Then let's get started!"

Everest grunted in agreement. He nodded in a random direction. Hurricane and Shade turned to see where he was looking. From behind a building, all the keepers and guides appeared. They walked towards the group.

"Air!" Hurricane shouted. He ran towards the winged she-cat.

Air grinned. "Long time no see, flight buddy!"

Hurricane laughed in his excitement.

"Water!" Shade barked happily. He shot forward and touched noses with the blue wolf. "You're back!"

"Shade!" Water barked back. She trotted towards him. She touched noses then stepped back. "How was your final quest?"

"Strangely not violent at all, but I'm not complaining, that's for sure! My pads bled a bit, though."

"Oh, are you okay?"

"Do we get any hellos?" woofed a green, brown and blue wolf. An orange, flaming she-cat stood beside her.

"Earth!" Hurricane and Shade said in unison. They ran over. "Earth! We haven't seen you since our first quest!"

Earth smiled. "I know."

The flaming orange she-cat beside her shuffled her paws. "Where's *my* hello?"

"Fire, we just saw you!" Hurricane laughed. "Do you need another hello?"

"It would be nice!" she laughed back.

"Okay, 'hello, Fire, it's been such a long time!' Happy?" Hurricane joked.

"This is all very nice, but we must begin the activation of the elements-" Everest was cut off by an excited mew.

"Hurricane! Shade!" screeched a black-and-white tuxedo kitten.

"Is that who I think it is?" Hurricane meowed loudly.

The kitten jumped at Hurricane and hit his broad chest. "Hurricane!"

"Eco!" Hurricane yowled. Shade gave a surprised bark and cantered over to nuzzle the little kitten. He squealed in delight.

"Shade!" Eco exclaimed. He jumped at Shade's furry chest. Shade lay down so that the kitten could pummel him playfully with his tiny paws. "You're both here!" He turned to Shade. "You still have the Earth Pouch I gave you!"

Shade looked down at the green pouch around his neck. "Of course I do! I couldn't get rid of it if I wanted to!" he laughed.

Everest barked to get everyone's attention. "Everyone! This is a very heartwarming reunion, but we must activate the elements. Now!"

Jay, Titus, and Bandit sprinted up to Shade and Hurricane and barreled them over, clearly unaware of what Everest had just said.

"Shade!" Jay half mewed, half roared. It was easy to forget that he was a tiger cub.

"Hurricane!" Titus yapped. He licked Hurricane's face all over. Hurricane didn't like it much, but he was too excited to care.

Everest was getting angry. He barked loudly so that the whole crowd quit talking. "I said, 'Now!'"

Shade and Hurricane scrambled up. They shook their former guides off of their backs and trotted towards Everest. "Alright. Fire, Air, Water, Earth, come here please." The keepers walked up. "Take off the Element Pouches." Each keeper took her own pouch off of the cat and dog. When Shade felt the ribbons being untied from his neck, he sighed in relief. It felt good to not have something hanging around his neck anymore, and Hurricane clearly felt the same.

Everest had each keeper set the pouches in a neat line in front of him. He took a deep breath and squinted his eyes shut. His muscles tensed, and his teeth ground together. He began to whisper soft words through his clenched teeth. The pouches began to glow.

Everyone watched intently as the embroidered letters on each pouch glowed brighter and brighter. Everest started trembling. The magic was a lot for him to handle.

A huge bang sounded behind the staring crowd. Everest kept his eyes closed. He seemed to be unaware of anything that was going on around him. The group turned their heads to where the noise had come from. There, snorting and heaving furious breaths, was the Dark Lord.

"You didn't think it would be that easy, did you?"

Chapter 50

It's funny how things happen. First, you're walking down the street; next, you've been swept into a whole new world, full of new opportunities. Your whole life can change in a split second. Whether it's for good or for bad, that's for you to decide.

"Than!" Hurricane yowled. "What are you doing here?"

"Did you idiots actually think that it would be as easy as that?" the Dark Lord sneered. "Of course not! There's no way that I would ever let you go like that! You will never have my life… or my world. This planet is mine, and mine for the keeping. You can't have it!"

"No!" Shade barked as loudly as his lungs and throat would allow. "This planet is not yours! The only ones that it belongs to are those who do good in this world and do not get swayed by self-interest or pride! You, Than, have gone beyond the boundaries of good! *Far* beyond! This planet belongs to you in no way, shape, or form!"

"I disagree. This world belongs to the ones who have power, strength, and no pity! Only the strongest will survive under my empire, which will leave me with a world full of strong warriors who will do all they can for my sake! I am the Dark Lord, the ruler of all I see!"

The Dark Lord raised his nose to the sky. "Attack!" Darkness consumed the twilight sky, and hundreds of Dark Force creatures poured over the tops of the buildings. The group gaped at the army, and immediately created a circle around Everest, who was still activating the elements. The guides huddled inside the circle, attempting to be fierce with small yaps and growls. Though, the only one that sounded the least bit fierce was Jay.

Spitting, hissing, barking and yowling erupted from the circle as the crowd tried to discourage the attack force. But their efforts were useless. The Dark Force army advanced on them quickly, coming closer with every terrified breath they took. Then the monsters were on them, growling and tearing at fur.

Shade took a frog-looking creature in his jaws and shook it forcefully. He threw the creature back into the crowd where it didn't get back up. But another took its place, and another after that. Hurricane swiped at the waves of creatures with furious hisses. But there were always more.

Air suddenly shot upward and dove down on the creatures, attacking them from above. That's when one jumped up in the air and dragged her down. Dozens of other creatures piled on top of her.

"No!" Hurricane yowled. He shot forward. "No!" Climbing over growling, screeching creatures, he fought his way to the pile. With enraged yowls and hisses, he dug through the pile, not caring about the hundreds of claws that seemed to be digging into his pelt. He got to the center of the pile and bucked, sending creatures flying. There was Air, heaving pained breaths. Her sides were bleeding, and her wings were crooked. "Air!" Hurricane urged. "Wake up! Don't die!"

Air opened her eyes halfway. She coughed, and stared at Hurricane, eyes wild with fear. Hurricane grabbed her scruff, and with a great bellow of pain, broke free from the trap of creatures. He dragged Air's body from the roaring crowd. Hurricane laid her down in the center of the circle. "Air? Are you okay?"

Air's eyes shot open. She gasped for breath, and shuffled her paws. "Hurricane?"

"Air!" he exclaimed, a bit relieved. He began to lick away bloodstains from her snow-white fur. The silver swirling pattern reappeared as he got rid of the red patches. He was able to make out where the cuts were, began to lick rapidly at them. The rest of the guides did the same, making the process a lot faster and easier.

When Hurricane saw that the guides had the job of licking the wounds closed under control, he began pumping at Air's chest, attempting to help her breathe. "Are you okay?"

Air didn't answer immediately. "Sort of," she rasped. At least she was responsive.

Hurricane sighed. "Good." He turned to the guides. "Help her. I swear, if I see any one of you outside the circle, it won't just be the Dark Forces who leave some bruises on you." The guides flinched, but obeyed.

Hurricane leapt into the roaring, screeching crowd. There weren't enough of them. He was constantly glancing back at the gasping form of Air. Would she make it?

"We need reinforcements!" Hurricane yowled as his wounds began to slow him down. "There are so many of them, and only five of us, excluding Air!"

Shade nodded, only to have his nod cut off as he clamped his jaws around the neck of yet another creature. "He's right! We'll all die if no one else helps us!"

Earth grunted in agreement and turned her head to Eco. "Eco! Get help!"

The little kitten looked up from Air. He looked small and vulnerable. His body shook with fear. But he succeeded in nodding. Earth shouted some Latin words, "*Reverto!*" She shouted the Latin word for "return". The kitten disappeared.

Time passed. Creatures kept coming like an endless flow of darkness. The sky was completely black, but the glow coming from the elements lit up the space. Air's breathing seemed to get stronger, but she still bled.

Then, they came. Battle cries erupted from the tops of the buildings, yowls and barks. Shade and Hurricane couldn't believe their eyes. There, atop the hill, each being led a by a Sighter, were two huge groups: the York Pack, and the Fletch Cat Club. The two crowds dropped into battle, fresh and ready to fight. Then, among the yowls and barks, came a chorus of howls. The circle of keepers and guides turned their heads toward the source of the noise. Only one animal could make such a beautiful sound: wolves! A huge pack of wolves poured out from the alleys, led by Eco and a Sighter Dog.

"You wanted help, and here they are!" Eco yowled. The wolves pounded through the surging Dark Force army like plows, and shook creatures in their jaws as though they were light as feathers. The army seemed to decrease in numbers as all three groups fought.

Shade searched the writhing multi-colored sea. There, in the midst of it all were Bailey and Snag, fighting back to back. Snag fought his way to the circle protecting Everest and Air.

"So you're more than just a dog, huh?" He barked between bites. "You never told me you were the savior!"

"I'm not the only one. It's me *and* Hurricane!"

Snag grunted. "Whatever." He dragged himself back into battle.

Shade decided to help Snag and Bailey. Leaping into the sea of darkness, he followed his bully. "What are you doing?" Snag barked out.

"Helping you!" Shade barked back. But before he could make another remark, claws sank into his sides. With an outcry of agony, he was dragged under a writhing, scratching pile of bodies. Shade was pushed into the center of the heap where every creature had a chance at clawing him. Within a few moments, he was completely submerged in the pile. No light could be seen, not even the brilliant glow of the elements as Everest activated them. Then the weight was lifted off of him, one by one. Light seeped through the flailing arms and legs.

"I need some help over here!" A voice barked out.

A few voices replied over the screeching of the war. Shade heard paws thundering over the asphalt to where he was being consumed by darkness. More weight was lifted, until finally, he could see faces. Five wolves created a circle around him, but only one spoke to him.

"Chosen one! You are the dog who was sent to find the... um, elements? Correct?"

Shade nodded, huffing. "Yes," he replied weakly. "I was one of two chosen to find the elements that would save the world."

The wolf nodded. "Right. Help him, you morons!" The four other wolves padded up and hoisted him onto one of their backs. A wolf supported him on each side. The two remaining wolves, the one that had spoken to him and another, kept watch at the front and back, biting and clawing at any creature that came too close. Shade almost fell off the back of the middle wolf in their haste to get back to the circle of guides and keepers. Finally, they dumped him next to Air.

"What's your name, chosen one?" The lead wolf asked.

Shade coughed. "It- it's Shade."

The wolf stared blankly at him. "What?"

"Shade," he said louder.

The wolf looked as though Shade had grown wings. "*Shade?*"

"Yeah. What, you think it's dumb?" Shade challenged.

"No. Not dumb at all." The wolf was gaping at him.

Only then did Shade recognize something about the wolf. The broad shoulders, the green eyes, the silvery-gray fur with brown touch-ups...

"Is your name... Rebel, by any chance?" Shade asked, ready to faint.

The wolf gasped. "Yes. Yes, it is."

Chapter 51

Shade couldn't believe his ears. "You are?"

Rebel reared up on his back paws in joy. "Yes! Shade! After all these years!"

Shade sprang to his paws. "*Dad?*"

"Yes!" Shade's father laughed in elation. He touched his nose to his son's. "Yes. This is beyond anything I could have imagined! My son is back!"

The other four wolves looked astonished. "*This* is your son?" one said.

Rebel whirled around. "Yes! He is!"

Hurricane turned and stared. "Your dad?"

Shade had forgotten that he was in the midst of battle from his amazement. "Dad!" Shade barreled his father over for the first time. He imagined that, once again, he was a pup. He pummeled his father's chest and nibbled on his ears playfully. His father laughed and laughed. He play-fought back. But the circle was so small that they rolled over Air.

She let out a mew. "Ow!"

Some of the guides had backed up against Earth and Water's paws. Seeing the lack of space, the four other wolves added themselves to the circle. Shade and Rebel stood, staring into each other's eyes.

"Where's Eclipse?" Rebel asked hopefully. "Is she with you?"

Shade's heart dropped. He could barely stand the fact that he had to tell his father the news. "She's not here."

"Then where is she?" Rebel was peering into the alleys of the surrounding buildings.

"I... I don't really know."

Rebel turned his head to his son. "What do you mean?"

A voice spoke up behind them. "She's not here." Shade turned to see Bailey's sad face. "She's in a puppy-mill."

"*What?*" Shade's father looked horrified. "She's where?"

"She was caught when I was about six months old," Shade informed. "Bailey is my half-sister. Eclipse was her mother too."

Rebel's head swung around. "Is she okay?" he asked Bailey. "Is she still there?"

Bailey hung her head. "I don't know."

Rebel sat staring at the ground. The battle raging around him seemed to mean nothing.

"She might be okay," Shade suggested hopefully. "Who knows?"

Rebel closed his eyes and shook his head hard. "It's fine. Forget it. We have a battle to win!" Rebel leapt over the head of Fire and dove back into the ocean of war. Shade followed.

A giant form rose from the black ground. "You shall not win!" the Dark Lord jabbed his staff in Shade's direction. More Latin words, as Earth had recited earlier, came from his mouth. "*Interficere!*" A red streak appeared from the ruby jewel at the tip. The streak shot at them like a lightning strike, but the Dark Lord was a few inches off. He instead hit one of the creatures. "No!" the Dark Lord roared. "*Interficere!*" he shouted again. Shade and Rebel dove away.

"Run!" Rebel ordered. Shade followed his father as they wove through the claws and teeth that attempted to wound them. Creatures, dogs, wolves and cats leaped through their path. The Dark Lord remained where he was, but kept shooting at them. He began to roar out the Latin word for "kill". "*Interficere!*"

Shade turned his head to where the Dark Lord raged. But as he looked, something else caught his eye. Snag was being pulled under. Rebel saw the dog as well, and ordered a few of his wolves to attack the dragon. As the wolves distracted the Dark Lord, Rebel and Shade ripped through the bodies of monsters to get to the bleeding form of Snag. A few dogs formed a circle around their injured leader. Shade and Rebel crouched near Snag's face. The burly dog was heaving. He could barely speak.

"Sh-Sh..." he coughed, "Shade?"

214

"Snag?" Shade asked. "Are you okay?"

Snag hacked and coughed. Blood trickled from his mouth. His eyes were half-closed and dull. Gashes covered his body, and they bled faster than anyone could prevent. One of his ears had been ripped painfully. The ear still stood straight, but what was left wasn't much.

"Shade... I'm sorry." Snag blinked back tears. This was the first time Shade had ever seen him cry.

"Sorry for what?" Shade asked as a lump formed in his throat.

"For everything," Snag admitted. "You never did anything wrong, yet I still treated you like you were nothing." Snag coughed again. More blood appeared. The sticky red liquid was staining Shade and Rebel's paws as Snag's wounds bled faster and faster. "You never asked to be half wolf... and... it's not a bad thing, either. You were treated like a coward by the rest of us, but you are not. You're a hero in the eyes of everyone, Shade. Be proud to hold the title," Snag coughed up more blood, "of 'wolf'." His eyes started to close. "Remember when you told me that you were in my junkyard to find your sister?"

Shade nodded and rested a paw on a gash in Snag's throat. He blinked back the tears that were streaming down his cheeks. The lump in his throat made it hard to speak. "Yes."

"It made me think of my brother," Snag choked out. His eyelids opened and his amber eyes shown. Memories twinkled in them. "We were best friends as pups, but were split up when a flood hit." Snag gave a small whimper of grief. "I never saw him again. He might be alive, but I'll never know." His eyes produced one more tear, and closed. "His name was Radcliff. My last wish," he declared with a gulp, "is for him to be okay. I'm sorry Shade." Snag drew in a ragged breath, and his flank stilled. Shade hung his head. His last moments with Snag had been spent settling their differences. Tears continued to stream down his face. His sadness was quickly replaced by rage. The Dark Lord had begun this war that had claimed Snag's life, and they would end it.

"Come on," Shade growled to his father. "Let's end this."

Shade and Rebel left the dogs to mourn their dead leader and went for Hurricane. They plowed through screeching Dark Forces until they arrived at the protection circle. Everest still stood with his eyes closed, activating the elements. *How long will this take?* Shade thought

Bailey stared at the section of the battlefield where Snag's motionless body lay. "He was never a fair leader, but he didn't deserve to die. There were times when he could be... good." Shade swallowed hard. Bailey was right. Snag had bullied him, but he had never wished death on him.

Shade turned to Hurricane. "I can't believe he's actually dead," Hurricane said, disbelievingly. "I never liked him, but he didn't deserve to *die.*"

Shade shook his head to clear it of the tears that were beginning to reform. "I know. He shouldn't have died, nobody deserves to die." He snapped his head in the direction of the Dark Lord. "Except, of course, him."

Hurricane looked in the same direction and nodded, snarling. "This battle is all his fault."

Bailey growled. "Agreed. Let's finish him!" letting out a battle cry, Bailey crashed through the protective circle. Shade, Hurricane, and Rebel followed. The circle quickly rebuilt itself.

"Attack!" Shade screeched. The others followed him, leaping onto the back of the Dark Lord. A few dogs, cats and wolves followed the action and jumped up on the dragon like a cowboy mounting a horse. The Dark Lord roared. "*Never!*" He pointed his staff at one of the cats, but thought better of it. He could hit himself. Instead, he took his free claw and swiped at the animals on his back. "Get *off!*" he bellowed. He started trying to buck them off. But they all sank their teeth and claws into his back, not only staying on, but inflicting pain as well. Win-win.

A few cats clawed their way over the wings and ripped through them with their claws. The Dark Lord cried out in frustration. He flapped his huge wings, hoping to throw them off. But they clung tightly.

Shade dismounted. Hurricane and Rebel followed, looking confused. "What are you doing?"

Shade pointed at the other attackers on Than's back. "They've got it under control. We need to protect Everest.

"Eve-who?" Rebel asked.

Hurricane flicked his tail. "It's a long story."

216

Shade looked at the circle of keepers and Rebel's four wolves. "They're protecting Everest. He's activating the elements that'll destroy the Dark Lord. Those are the things that we went on a big quest for."

"Oh," Rebel replied, still looking a bit confused.

"We'll explain it all later. Promise. Let's go." Shade twisted around and advanced on the circle. Once they were there, the light coming from the elements almost blinded them. "Wow," Shade gasped, squinting. He turned his back to the pouches and added himself to the circle. Shade faced the warring monsters, wolves, cats and dogs. He would protect Everest, Air, and the elements with his life.

Chapter 52

The battle seemed to be slowing. The animals on their side looked tired. The Dark Lord had shaken the wolves, cats and dogs off of his back and disappeared. The elements were glowing so brightly now that they lit up everything as bright as day that was within three city blocks. Everest kept whispering and tensing.

The creatures kept coming and coming. They were being controlled by some voice; Shade suspected it was the Dark Lord. If the elements could just begin their... magical powers, perhaps they would destroy the Dark Lord and the creatures would retreat. *What is Everest doing?* Shade thought as he bit and scratched...

Everest walked through the corridors of dark, endless caves. The Great Defender of the Elements had to be here somewhere. The world would soon be destroyed. "Great Element Defender! Please! Show yourself! You must help us!" Everest was answered only by his echo. He hung his head. Where was the Defender? He pressed his forehead against one of the stone walls. Thinking hard, he panted. He was getting tired and lost. But he couldn't open his eyes yet. Everest had to find him. Taking a deep breath, he chose a path and took it. His paw steps echoed around him, and his faint shadow was his only companion. Suddenly, his good eye saw light ahead. Candlelight. Was this the throne room of the Great Defender of the Elements? He walked faster and faster until the entrance to the cave was right around the corner.

He turned the rounded corner and looked through the entrance. A huge cavern met his gaze. The floor of the cavern was covered in a blue velvet carpet. Leading to a gold and red throne was a long red carpet with gold trim. A red curtain, like the ones on stages, circled the throne. There, sitting on the beautiful throne, was the Great Defender of the Elements. He was a lion with a magnificent golden mane. Deep brown eyes blinked at Everest. On either side, long tables filled with delicious food made his nose twitch. Chickens, roasts, salads, steaks, cheeses, cakes, breads, sandwiches, more food than you could imagine. Also, on each table, dozens of candles were lit. Above, the gray rocks of the cave were still there, and stalactites hung down, but a huge chandelier twinkled as even more candle flames licked at the air.

Everest walked up to the Element Defender and bowed low. "Great Defender of the Elements. I am honored to be in your presence."

"As am I," the deep voice replied. It was the deepest voice Everest had heard, even deeper than the Dark Lord's. The strength of that voice gave Everest the courage to meet the great lion's gaze. He saw in those eyes wisdom and kindness. "I already know why you have come to see me." He held up a huge paw to halt his explanation. "You have worked hard to find me through these great caves. You have much patience, Everest. In return, I will help you. Come. A battle has begun."

Fear sliced through Everest like a knife. "It has?"

The Element Defender nodded slowly, closing his eyes. "Yes. Come, we shall help them. I will activate the elements for you."

"Thank you!" Everest exclaimed, relieved. The massive cat rose from his throne, his great mane waving. Everest's two red and blue feathers swished as the lion jumped down, sending air blasting forward. The Element Defender pointed his nose to the cave ceiling. "*Reverto!*" He shouted the Latin word. With a *bang*, the scene was gone...

Shade batted at a creature weakly. His strength was nearly gone, and he panted hard. In his lack of force, another creature jumped at his throat and clamped down hard. Shade let out a cry of torment. Blood spurted out from beneath the creature's merciless jaws. The pain shot throughout his neck and throat. Red liquid leaked from his mouth. A black haze covered his vision as the creature clamped down harder. Seeing his son in trouble, Rebel vaulted forward and tore the creature off. The gash in Shade's throat made it hard to breathe, and he hacked up more blood.

"Help!" Rebel shouted. Shade tried to swallow, but it only made his throat sting. He started to panic. Breathing was getting gradually more difficult. Hurricane ran over and pressed his paws on Shade's throat. The bleeding lessened. Air flopped over.

"Give him these." She held out a paw. On it were three white feathers. "They fell off where my wings were broken. Put them on the gash in his throat. It'll stop the bleeding."

Hurricane took Air's wing feathers and pressed them to Shade's throat. "There. That should help." Hurricane pushed a piece of fur from his eyes. The bleeding decreased. "It's working!" Hurricane exclaimed.

Rebel let out a sigh of relief. He looked in satisfaction where the creature lay motionless.

Suddenly, with a flash of light, Everest's eye opened. It cast a blue glow, and he shook as though an earthquake had just hit. A lion appeared beside him. The big cat had to sit down because of the lack of space. The guides ran under Rebel's paws to create more room. The elements sent a blast of light as bright as the sun across the battlefield. The Dark Lord reappeared. "No! Not now! Not when I'm so close!"

Shade stood, shakily, on his paws. He met the Dark Lord's gaze bravely. Hurricane did the same.

"It's your time to go, Than," Hurricane growled. *You've caused enough trouble.*

Shade coughed, but managed to speak. "You've done enough."

Everest blinked, and the ray of blue coming from his eye ceased. "Goodbye, Dark Lord."

The lion next to Everest let out a huge roar. It echoed throughout the surrounding buildings. The elements lifted out of their pouches. They shone brightly, and levitating higher, still, into the air. They cast a brilliant light on the battle. Many of the creatures screeched and retreated.

"What are you doing?" the Dark Lord roared to his fleeing army. "Fight them, you cowards! I am your ruler! You do as I say!" The Dark Forces didn't listen. They kept streaming out of the city.

The elements shot rays of light down at the group. Shade's gash stopped bleeding, as did Air's wounds. The wounds of the wolves, cats and dogs that had fought against Dark Forces stopped bleeding as well, though the wounds themselves did not disappear. Shade was glad that no more blood was spilling down his chest or chin.

The elements started spinning. As they spun faster, a huge wind blasted everyone's fur. Then, the elements crashed into each other. They stilled, and then advanced on the Dark Lord. The huge black and red dragon fell on his back and covered his face. "No!" He pleaded. He pointed his staff at the ball of light. "*Defluo!*" He shouted the Latin word for "disappear".

The ball of light did not disappear. It spun faster. Finally, the ball was shooting towards Than, and when it hit him, there was a burst of light. The force of the explosion sent everyone flying backwards. They tumbled across the road. When the light stopped, all that was left was a huge cloud of dust. Color had returned to the sky. Everyone looked up, expecting the Dark Lord to appear from the cloud, flying at him or her in increased rage. But the cloud only rolled and dispersed. Once the cloud had cleared, nothing was there. Nothing but... a staff.

Shade's eyes widened in complete amazement. The Dark Lord was gone.

Hurricane felt the tingle of astonishment creep through his belly. A chill went up his spine as he wondered where the Dark Lord was. He walked towards the staff, almost too scared to touch it. The red ruby jewel glowed faintly. The lion walked up behind him.

"I understand you are all wondering who I am." The lion waited as everyone nodded and muttered, still dazed from their sudden victory. The lion lowered his head in greeting. "I am the Great Defender of the Elements. The elements are my responsibility to keep safe." The Element Defender walked over to where the Element Pouches still lay. "These are mine," he declared respectfully. He called Eco over. "Please, tie these around my neck."

"But your neck's too big," Eco pointed out.

The Element Defender laughed and stomped a paw on the ground. "*Amplus!*" He roared the Latin word for "large". The ribbons on each pouch suddenly expanded to his length. Eco blinked. He tied each ribbon around the Element Defender's neck. The Element Defender stood up. "Thank you for keeping these ancient pouches safe," he said to Shade and Hurricane. "You are worthy of the title of 'hero'." The lion roared into the sky and disappeared.

Shade and Hurricane looked at each other and smiled. Then, like a song, Rebel held his head to the rising moon. He howled their victory to the appearing stars. The sun set in the distance. The rest of Rebel's wolves pointed their noses to the moon and howled along with him. The dogs of the York Pack barked and howled along with the wolves. Soon, the Fletch Cat Club caught on and began to yowl at the stars. Soon the night was filled with victorious howls, yowls and barks. Hurricane closed his eyes and yowled with his friends. Then, for the first time in his life, Shade howled at the moon.

The night was beautiful, and the stars shone brighter than ever before. A huge group of dogs showed up. Everest turned his head to the dogs. Each dog in the group had a red feather and a blue feather behind their ears. Following them was a group of cats with the same red and blue feathers.

"Sighters!" Everest greeted them with a happy bark. "What about the Rocky Mountain Sighter Meeting?"

"It can wait," answered Rocky.

Aurora walked up behind him. "Yes. This is much more important. Where is the Dark Lord?"

"Gone!" Hurricane exclaimed. "We defeated him!"

Aurora and Rocky gasped. "*Gone*?"

"Yes," Everest replied. "We fought for a long time. But good always wins."

Aurora and Rocky laughed in agreement. "Then let us celebrate!" The Sighters joined in the yowling, barking and howling. They had won.

Epilogue

Shade sat next to his father. They were on the edge of the forest and the city.

Hurricane walked up next to them. He looked up at Shade with sad, yet hopeful, bright blue eyes. "Are you sure you want to go?"

"I'll visit," Shade promised. "I'm just a while away. It's not like I'm leaving forever." Shade looked back at the city. The buildings twinkled in noon light. "The city will always be a part of me. I'm still half dog, remember?"

Hurricane nodded. "Yeah. You better visit, or I'll come get you!" Hurricane jumped at him. Even though he wasn't strong enough to actually push Shade over, Shade toppled onto his side playfully. The black tomcat nibbled Shade's ears, and Shade batted at him softly.

Rebel looked up at the sun. "Time to go. Say your last goodbyes, Shade."

Shade stood up. He walked over to where Bailey and Deacon stood. He rested his head on Deacon's shoulders. "I'll miss the bar."

Deacon laughed. "That's why, when ya' visit Hurricane and Bailey here, ya' stop by!"

Shade smiled. "I will." He turned to his sister. She wouldn't look at him.

"Do you have to go?" She asked. "Ever since the York Pack broke up again, I don't have a group." She looked at him with pleading eyes. "I had hoped that you would stay with me. You're my brother. Siblings need to stick together."

Shade and Rebel shared a look. "Well, that's why I want to ask you something: will you come with me?"

Bailey blinked. "What?"

"Rebel and I talked it over. He said that you could join the wolf pack, too."

"Oh, Shade! I don't know…"

"I'm the alpha male," Rebel pointed out. "No one will be allowed to argue. You may not be my true daughter, but I would be more than willing to take you in as though you were. You're my son's sister."

Bailey looked back at the city. "Could I think about it?"

Rebel thought a moment. "I'll give you a week or two. Is that enough?"

Bailey nodded. "Yes, that should be enough."

Rebel smiled. "Okay. We'll come for you then." Rebel looked at his son. "Come on. It's time for you to meet your family."

"Where's our goodbye?" a voice asked. Everyone turned around.

"Air!" Hurricane exclaimed. Lexie, who had been sitting next to Hurricane, gave Air a strange look. Was that jealousy?

"Water! Earth! Fire!" Shade ran to the keepers. He touched noses to each one. "It's so good to see you all!" He turned his eyes to where Air spoke to Hurricane. "How is she doing?"

Earth answered. "Her wounds have healed nicely. Her flight is getting much better as well."

"Great!" Shade cheered. "Everyone else?"

"We're all fine."

Shade turned his gaze. "Everest!" The old dog stood smiling. His eye-patch looked shiny. "Is that a new one?"

Everest chuckled. "Yes. The other one was getting worn out. How are you doing, Shade? Hurricane, how are you?"

"I'm good," Hurricane answered.

"Me too," echoed Shade.

"I understand you've decided to leave your city life? A big step. Are you sure that's what you want to do, Shade?" Everest tilted his head questioningly.

Shade nodded vigorously. "Yes. I'm sure."

Everest leaned forward and whispered in Shade's ear. "I'll take you and Hurricane to the next Rocky Mountain Sighter Meeting, okay?"

"Okay," Shade replied. He shuffled the newly fallen snow at his paws. It was soft and glinted in the noon sun. Clouds in the west threatened to bring more.

Lastly, four bundles of fur threw themselves at Shade. "Eco! Titus! Jay! Bandit!" The puppies, kitten and cub climbed all over Shade.

They yipped and mewed in joy. "Do you *have* to leave?" "When will you be back?" "You'll come back, right?" "Will we have any more adventures?"

Shade answered each question. "Yes, I don't know, yes, and maybe."

"Okay!" They all said at once, and continued to barrel over Hurricane.

"Alright, Shade. No more stalling. The pack will be waiting." Rebel began to pad through the snow.

Shade looked at the group. "I'll visit. Don't forget about me." A lump was forming in his throat. He could tell everyone else felt the same. "Bye, everyone!" He followed his father until the two of them were lost among the trees.

Hurricane sat down with a thump. "He's gone."

"Not forever," Everest reminded him. *He'll be back. Shade will always have part of this city in his heart. He has a destiny big enough for ten dogs. He's not gone, that's for sure. He'll never be alone either. I'll always be watching.*

Always.

15694263R00128

Made in the USA
San Bernardino, CA
03 October 2014